"Goodbye, Celia," Eric said, his voice rasping almost below register.

She swallowed. "Bye," she whispered.

His sapphire eyes glittered with something lost and sad and so hungry that Celia felt her own body shaking with the need to fill it. For a long moment she felt suspended in that painful, jeweled gaze. Then he let her go an inch at a time, until somehow they were standing separate again, facing each other in the bright light of a Texas morning.

He hitched his pack onto one shoulder and strode off down the muddy road without a backward glance. Celia watched him, her heart pounding. She was glad she had kissed him, that she would always carry the memory of it.

Because she would never see him again. And considering everything, that was probably a very good thing. A man like that . . .

Setting her jaw, she turned back to the work that awaited her. Her life had been filled with dangerous turns and instability. A man like that would only bring more of the same. . . .

Dear Reader,

Welcome to Silhouette **Special Edition** . . . welcome to romance. Each month Silhouette **Special Edition** publishes six novels with you in mind—stories of love and life, tales that you can identify with—as well as dream about.

And this December brings six wonderful tales of love! Sherryl Woods's warm, tender series, VOWS, concludes with Brandon Halloran's romance— *Cherish*. Brandon finally meets up again with his first love, beautiful Elizabeth Forsythe. Yes, Virginia, as long as there is life and love, dreams *do* come true!

Heralding in the Christmas spirit this month is *It Must Have Been the Mistletoe* by Nikki Benjamin. This winsome, poignant story will bring a tear to your eye and a smile to your lips!

Rounding out this month of holiday cheer are books from other favorite writers: Trisha Alexander, Ruth Wind, Patricia Coughlin and Mona van Wieren.

I hope that you enjoy this book and all the stories to come. Happy holidays from all of us at Silhouette Books!

Sincerely,

Tara Gavin
Senior Editor
Silhouette Books

P.S.—We've got an extra special surprise next month to start off the New Year right. I'll give you a hint—it begins with a wonderful book by Ginna Gray called *Building Dreams!*

RUTH WIND

JEZEBEL'S BLUES

Silhouette

SPECIAL ▼ EDITION®

Published by Silhouette Books New York

America's Publisher of Contemporary Romance

For the blue-eyed, gorgeous, legendary Putmans; especially Madoline O'Neal Putman, who gave me the magic of Texas in her stories. Thanks, Grandma.

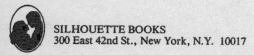

SILHOUETTE BOOKS
300 East 42nd St., New York, N.Y. 10017

JEZEBEL'S BLUES

Copyright © 1992 by Barbara Samuel

ISBN: 0-373-09785-9

First Silhouette Books printing December 1992

Printed in the U.S.A.

Books by Ruth Wind

RUTH WIND

has been addicted to books and stories for as long as she can remember. When she realized at the age of seven that some lucky people actually spent their days spinning tales for others, she knew she had found her calling. The direction of that calling was decided when the incurable romantic fell in love with the films *Dr. Zhivago* and *Romeo and Juliet*.

The Colorado native holds a bachelor's degree in journalism and lives with her husband and two young sons at the foot of the Rockies.

OKLAHOMA

ARKANSAS

NEW MEXICO

Ft. Worth

Dallas

LOUISIANA

Gideon

Jezebel River

Waco

Austin

Houston

TEXAS

MEXICO

Corpus Christi

Gulf of Mexico

All underlined places are fictitious.

Prologue

It wasn't a big river. Mainly it ran sleepily and quietly through a sparsely populated stretch of farmland in east Texas. Fishermen angled for the catfish skimming its depths; young boys stripped and skinny-dipped in its pools; lovers picnicked on its banks.

Only a handful of old-timers remembered the old name for the sleepy river—a name murmured in hushed voices as stories were told of her power.

Jezebel.

Not the Jezebel River. Just Jezebel, a name reserved for women of lusty beauty and uncertain virtue. *Jezebel.*

There had only been one occasion in recent memory when Jezebel had awakened, like an aging courtesan, to remind those around her of the power she could wield. Only one life was lost that night, and as if placated by the sacrifice, Jezebel settled back into her sleep.

But the old-timers knew it was only a matter of time until she awakened once again to flash her eyes and spread her skirts.

Only a matter of time.

Chapter One

Not even hell could be so dark. His car headlights poked white fingers into the heavy rain, barely penetrating. The wiper blades sluiced the water away at a furious pace. It wasn't enough. Only square inches of the windshield were clear at any instant—as soon as the blades slogged away the rain, more fell to blur his vision once again.

He'd slowed to twenty on the back country road and was no longer intimately familiar with the twists of blacktop and the tiny bridges that spanned dozens of creeks. His fingers ached from gripping the steering wheel. He hunched as far forward in his seat as he could go, trying vainly to see.

Storm warnings had been broadcast on the radio, of course. But he'd grown up in these thick woods, amid the floods and endless early-summer rains. He knew the television and radio people were prone to exaggeration. It sold papers and commercial time.

The car slid on the road, its tires unable to keep a grip on the pavement. Eric swore as he fought for control. It made sense to ignore the news people, but he probably ought to have listened to the boy in grease-stained overalls at the gas station twenty miles back.

But there was his pride to consider. Nothing scared him like driving in the rain, in the dark. A night like this had once shattered his life, and he knew instinctively that he would be truly lost if he let the fear overtake him tonight.

Doggedly, he kept driving. A green sign with reflective white letters flashed in front of his lights. The words blurred before Eric could read them, but he knew what the sign said: Gideon, 5 miles. Almost there. With the back of his wrist, he wiped the sweat from his brow. For once in his life, he wished he'd paid attention—he'd have been a whole lot better off staying overnight in a motel in the last town. He sure as hell couldn't do much for his sister if he drowned out here.

His headlights picked out a wash of water pouring over a bridge just ahead. A new row of sweat beads broke out on his upper lip and he eased his foot from the accelerator. Sucking in his breath, he touched the brake. Easy, he told himself. His weakened fingers, slick with sweat, slid on the hard, plastic steering wheel.

In spite of his care, the car hit the water with a hollow sounding *thunk. Easy now.* It wasn't the first creek he'd forded on this nightmarish trip. Every little trickle in the county was brimming over tonight.

But this one had more than bubbled over. Eric saw the nearby pond with which the stream had mated, and the offspring of their union looked like an inland sea. Through the side window of the car, he saw an unbroken span of water reflecting the oddly misplaced light of a farmer's barn.

The engine spluttered and coughed. Died. He slammed his good hand against the dash. When the car swayed under the force of the water that rose over its fenders, fear squeezed his belly hard. No time to brood.

He reached over the back of the seat, grabbing the heavy canvas backpack that held most of his earthly goods. Next to it was a guitar in a black case. He hesitated, fingers curled around the slim, plastic handle. A shiver of water shook the car.

He let go. It was no good to him anymore, anyway.

It took a mighty heave to get the door open and then the water nearly knocked him down. Another flash of adrenaline sizzled over his nerves. Falling rain soaked his head and body in seconds. Shifting the backpack on his shoulders, he sloshed forward, head down. A big, broken tree branch swirled by him on the current.

Scared, man?

Damned right, he answered himself, putting one foot determinedly in front of the other. As he gained the other side of the bridge, the water gradually receded until it just covered the bottoms of his feet.

The little triumph pleased him. Only five miles to Gideon, to his sister, the only person in the world who mattered to him. And she needed him. It was bound to be easier to get to her on foot than in the car. So he ignored the beckoning lights of the farmhouse set back in the heavy trees and pushed onward into the thick, rainy darkness.

He trudged a mile. Two. He lost track. He crossed one stream, sloshing through water up to his knees, and when he got to the other side, he found the stream came with him, up to his ankles.

He thought about going back to the farmhouse, shook his head, and pushed on.

One foot in front of the other. Water obscured the road, making it hard to keep his bearings. He paused once to peer into the darkness, trying to mark familiar spots. There were none.

He reached into his backpack for a bottle of Jack Daniel's and slugged back a considerable mouthful. It warmed his chilled insides, calmed his racing heart. Thus fortified, he replaced the bottle, wiped water from his eyes and started out again. Not far now.

Celia Moon was making popcorn when the lights suddenly failed. For several hours she'd been trying to resist food—since the rains had set in several days ago, her main activity had been eating. But the pervasive thought of butter and salt and fluffy white corn had proved impossible to resist.

The sudden failure of the lights seemed like a scolding from on high—but not even heaven could make her quit now. There was enough heat left in the electric burner to finish the popping. The butter was already melted and the bowl was ready. If she had to sit alone in the gloomy darkness of the old farmhouse, reading by candlelight, at least she'd have some buttered popcorn to comfort herself with.

Working easily in the dark, she pulled the bowl over as the bubbling sound of exploding kernels slowed, then lifted the heavy pan from the stove and aimed as well as she could. There would doubtless be popcorn strewed all over the table in the morning, but since she lived alone, what did it really matter?

She did need a light to pour the butter. There were candles in a drawer by the sink and Celia lit one. A piney scent rose from the plump green candle and mixed with the smell of hot popcorn.

The whole elaborate ritual was designed to be a distraction from the endless pattering of the rain on the roof and windows. Endless. "A hurricane caught in a holding pattern over the Gulf," they had said on the news. Rain was forecast for tomorrow as well.

It was depressing. She'd been stuck inside the house for days, cleaning like a madwoman out of boredom when she should have been planting her first garden. A salad garden to start with, scallions and radishes and lettuce. Collards, maybe. Definitely popcorn. Her grandmother had always grown popcorn, sending big bags of it every fall to Celia in Brussels or Paris or Berlin, wherever her parents' travels had taken them.

A sudden, urgent pounding on the front door crashed into the rain-framed silence. Celia started, sending butter spilling over the whole table. She scowled at the mess. The knock sounded again, louder this time.

Who in the world would be out on such a night? She headed for the door, shaking her head, then realized she couldn't see anything without her candle and went back for it. The pounding rattled through the room again.

"I'm coming," she muttered under her breath. She grabbed a handful of popcorn as she picked up the candle, then ran lightly toward the door, her candle flame bobbing with her steps.

She flung open the door—and nearly flung it just as quickly closed.

The man on the porch was soaking wet. No, not just soaking. Dripping. Awash. Streams flowed from the pack on his shoulders and from his hair. A cut on his lip was bleeding profusely, and he was panting. "I—got—stranded," he managed to say, and stumbled forward, catching himself on the doorjamb.

Celia jumped back, alarmed. It was impossible to see much about him by the light of her single candle, but he was big. A stranger. He also smelled distinctly of whiskey.

He straightened and licked his lips. "I was trying to get to town, but that last creek nearly took me with it."

Celia hesitated a moment more—measuring the weight of the storm against the big man who obviously wanted shelter. His voice, ragged and hoarse, was definitely local, with a certain, unmistakable cadence that marked him as a native. She didn't think she'd ever seen him, but that didn't mean much. She'd only been in town a few months, and small as it was, Gideon played county seat to a lot of farms.

She stepped back. "My grandmother would never forgive me for turning away a stranger in trouble. Come on in."

The relief on his face, even in the dark, was unmistakable. "Much obliged. I won't be any trouble."

"Wet as you are, I'll be lucky if you don't die of pneumonia before morning." She sized him up, thinking quickly. "Stay right there. I'll get you something dry to put on."

"You don't have to do that," he protested.

"Don't be ridiculous." She headed for the back room, leaving the candle for him. He hovered near the door.

There wasn't much to choose from, but Celia found an old pair of overalls of her grandfather's and a shirt she was sure would be too small. Might not fit well, but it would be better than freezing to death.

The stranger still stood right by the door when she returned. A puddle had formed under his feet. His outer garment, a long vinyl poncho, had been shed, and the big pack rested against the wall.

The lights flashed on again, so suddenly they startled Celia. In the blazing, unexpected illumination, she stared at the man by the door. It was only by sheer force of will that she kept her mouth from dropping open. Men like this never walked into her quiet life. They crossed movie screens and album covers; they rode bucking horses in rodeos and raced cars in the Indy.

They didn't appear on her porch in rural Texas in the middle of a rainstorm.

His hair was black as sin and already curling around his neck and ears. The face was broad and dark, with high cheekbones and heavy brows over thick-lashed eyes. Amid all the masculine angles and jutting corners, his mouth was uncommon and compelling, even with a bloody cut obscuring it. The lower lip was full, sensual; the upper cut into an exquisite firm line.

There was only an instant for her to absorb the lines of his body, for the lights flashed off as quickly as they'd come on.

She laughed a little breathlessly, not quite sure whether the sound stemmed from excitement or fear. "Well, that was fast. I wonder if we're going to be treated to a light show."

"Somebody at the plant better get smart quick and turn everything off," he said, "or there's likely to be fires all over the county."

The man shivered and Celia hurriedly gave him the clothes. "I'll wait in the kitchen."

Standing there in the dark, nibbling popcorn from the bowl on the table, she wondered if she was completely insane. The world was not the same place her grandmother had lived in, although Celia supposed there had always been serial killers and rapists roaming the countryside. Computers had just made it simpler to track them down. The thought made her smile briefly.

The stranger's voice, with its odd edge of roughness, sounded directly behind her. "Jezebel's acting up tonight," he said.

"Jezebel?" Celia echoed, turning.

He'd brought the candle with him, and the light cast eerie shadows over the hollows of his face. She saw a grizzling of dark beard on his chin and top lip. It added an even more rakish appearance to his rugged face. Celia frowned at the blood on his mouth. "You're bleeding," she said, and reached into a drawer for a dishcloth.

Distractedly, he pressed the cloth to the cut, then lifted it and licked the spot experimentally. "I didn't even feel this," he commented.

Celia lifted the candle closer to his face, and understanding her intention, he lowered the dishrag. "You probably need a stitch or two," she said. "But it looks like you'll have to live without them until morning."

"I've lived through worse."

There was no boast in the words, just a simple statement of fact. Celia realized she was still standing next to him, the candle held aloft, peering at his face for clues to his nature like the heroine in a Gothic novel. She put the candle on the table. "Who's Jezebel?" she asked.

"The river. That's what the old-timers call her."

"Why?"

"Because," the man said, cocking his head a bit ironically, "she's as dangerous as a faithless and beautiful woman." He spied the popcorn and pointed. "You mind?"

"Help yourself." Celia ladled up a handful for herself. "Pretty sexist. Why isn't she like a faithless man?"

A slow grin spread over his face. "Because no man alive can outsmart a wise and evil woman—and the old-timers knew it."

His voice, low and husky, acted like moonshine on her spine, easing the muscles all the way down. She straightened. "What makes you think she's acting up?"

"I've seen her do it." He glanced toward the window, as though the river was a banshee about to scream through the night. "Unless it stops raining right now, she's coming."

Celia frowned and crossed to the window. It was dark—inky dark. The pond in the hollow had crept up another four or five inches, and she thought she could see a fine film of water all over the saturated ground. "It's been flooding for weeks," she said. "Everyone says that happens every year."

"They like to forget about old Jezebel." He shifted. "Legends aside, this is a flood plain, and the river runs in cycles. She's gonna flood and you'd best be on high ground when she does."

"There's an attic here if I need it."

He scooped up another big handful of popcorn. "Is it stocked?"

She shrugged. "Sort of." She pursed her lips. "Do you think the river's going to overflow tonight?"

He wandered to the window, and as he stood next to her, looking out at the rain, Celia realized he was much, much larger than she. What if all this talk of a flood was just a way to get her up into the attic to ravish her or something? She crossed her arms over her chest, smelling whiskey and something deeper, a scent of hot nights that she tried to ignore. There was no law that said serial killers were ugly and hard to get along with. In fact, how did any of them get close to their victims unless they possessed a certain—well, animal magnetism that promised erotic rewards in return for trust?

But his voice was so very grim when he spoke again that Celia had no doubt that he was telling the truth. "She's coming," he said, the dread in his voice unmistakable.

Suddenly, from the depths of childhood came a memory. Celia had awakened thirsty and padded into the bathroom for a drink of water. On her way back to her room, she heard her father in his office, shouting into the phone. Curious and alarmed, she had paused by the door.

Her father had been a big man, as big as a grizzly, he liked to tell her. That night he hunched in the swivel chair by his desk, with his hair wild and his face buried in his hands. "What's wrong, Daddy?" Celia asked.

He turned in his chair and gestured for her to come sit in his lap. Then, because it had been his policy to tell Celia the truth, he said, "There's a flood back in Texas and I can't get through to make sure Grandma's all right."

Celia didn't really understand anything else about the incident, but obviously, Grandma had been fine. She'd only died last year—in her sleep.

Thinking of it now, though, she realized the river had probably flooded then. "Okay," she said, taking a breath. "Jezebel's going to flood. Since you're here, you can help me lug things up to the attic.'' She crossed the room, taking the candle with her, and opened the oak cupboard by the sink.

"What happened to the old woman, Mrs. Moon, who used to live here?'' the stranger asked as Celia took cans and boxes from the shelf.

"She died last year.'' Celia flashed him a grin out of proportion to his statement. Relief made her sigh. If he had known her grandmother, he wasn't likely to be a serial killer.

"Are you kin?''

"I'm her granddaughter. She left me the house.''

He nodded, chewing popcorn. "What's your name, granddaughter?''

"Celia.'' She glanced at the nearly empty bowl. "You made short work of that popcorn. Are you hungry?''

"Celia Moon.'' His drawl and the ragged edge of his voice made her name sound beautiful. "I'm Eric Putman and I'm starving.''

She tossed him a box of crackers and found the peanut butter. "That'll have to do for a little while.'' His name sounded vaguely familiar, but when she couldn't place it, she let it go. There weren't many names she hadn't heard on her grandmother's lips at one time or another. For a nice old woman, she'd been the world's champion gossip—not mean, for there was always an undercurrent of understanding in the way she told her stories, even when the preacher of the Methodist church fell in love with the choir director, who was then only seventeen, and ran off to Louisiana with her. "You must be from around here," Celia commented.

"Born and raised."

A harsh undernote told her he'd been glad to escape. A common attitude. She was the only one who'd run to Gideon instead of away. And the funny thing was, they were running to the very places she had left behind, places whose very names promised glamour. "You've been gone awhile," she said.

"Yep." He dropped the peanut butter and crackers into the box with the other food. "You have any other candles? I can get some blankets and stuff if you'll tell me where to look."

She dug in a drawer, and just as she was about to light the candle, a massive flash of lightning shimmered over the sky, a pale electric blue that seemed to hang for minutes in the darkness. On its heels came a crack of thunder so loud, it rattled the dishes.

As if a hole had been cut in the sky by the violent thunder, the noise of the rain suddenly doubled, then tripled. Celia gasped. "I didn't think it could rain any harder!" She went to the window and looked out, laughing lightly. "It looks like there's a thousand garden hoses going at once."

Eric grabbed the candle. "Where are those blankets?" His voice was gruff.

"Under the stairs." She pointed vaguely. Her attention was focused on the deluge. It excited her. A part of her wanted to run outside into that beating, pounding rain, just to feel it and taste it. Nature run amok, she thought. Humans were helpless in the face of it. A savage kind of joy raced through her at the thought.

"Come on, woman," Eric growled. "Won't take Jezebel long to flash her eyes now."

Of course, she probably wanted to *live* through whatever was coming. Time enough to observe the drama when everything was safely prepared.

Celia tried to ignore the ripple of excitement that passed through her at the thought of observing the drama with Eric Putman nearby.

Chapter Two

It took more than an hour to prepare the attic. They made several trips up and down the long flight of stairs, carrying water and blankets and food. Eric insisted they drag up a mattress from one of the beds, and evidently Celia finally understood the gravity of the situation, because she gathered a box full of photo albums and letters, and a metal file box he assumed held important papers of various kinds.

Eric's last trip was to fetch his backpack and shoes, which he'd left downstairs when he changed.

Water was seeping in under the front door. Feeling the cold water on his bare toes, Eric froze for an instant. A paralyzing fear shot through his belly, and his mind flashed back to that other night, so long ago, when the water had crept under the front door and up the windowpanes—until the pressure shattered the windows, and water had rocketed through the openings. There had been no attic in that house, only a roof to cling to. He'd clung. Sometimes he could still taste the silt in his mouth, feel the slime on his arms and under his feet.

Flood. Jezebel was rising. Down the hall, the toilet gurgled ominously. Staring at the water pushing through the crack below the door, he knew what he had to do. First he grabbed the bottle in his pack and lifted it for a long swallow. Then he crossed the room and yanked open the door.

A cold press of waiting water swirled inside, rushing across the floor all the way to the couch against the far wall. Gritting his teeth, he sloshed through it to the windows. Methodically, trying not to look at the sea beyond the house, he rounded the lower floor, opening all the windows.

He returned to the foot of the stairs and paused a moment, holding his candle aloft. The room was as warm and inviting as a June morning. Wallpaper with tiny blue-and-silver flowers covered one wall, and an arrangement of framed botanical drawings hung above the fat, rose-colored sofa. Small tables littered with magazines and knickknacks and lamps were scattered around the room. Eric let his eyes rove from one corner to the other, imprinting in memory what would soon be swept away, then he hiked his pack onto his shoulder and climbed the stairs.

Celia was crouched by the window tucked under the eaves of the attic, a single candle burning nearby. He was struck again by her fey beauty, so fitting to her name. Everything about her was as ethereal as moonlight. Her hair was fine and weightless, so blond it was nearly white, and skimmed her fragile-looking shoulders in a straight line. She wasn't short, but her body was slim of breast and hip, and she had long-fingered, graceful hands.

But downstairs, when the lights had flashed on suddenly, it had been her eyes that riveted him, in spite of the fact that they'd been filled at that moment with fear and distrust.

Never had he seen a face so dominated by eyes. They were enormous, fringed with lashes unusually dark for one with such light hair, and the irises were pale gray, almost silver.

Fey.

Now he saw more—a mouth as ripe as peaches and a pointed, stubborn chin. He grinned, feeling relieved. She was just a woman, not some specter from another plane. "Some rain, eh?" he said with a grin.

"Amazing. I've never seen anything like it." She frowned. "Are you nipping at a bottle? You smell like whiskey."

"Guilty." He tugged the fifth of Jack Daniel's from his pack. It was nearly full. "I carry it for emergencies."

She wryly glanced out the window. "This qualifies, I guess."

"You want a little?"

"I hate whiskey," she said bluntly. "Go ahead, though, if it makes you feel better."

"No." He put it away.

An awkward silence fell. Eric dug into his pack for oranges and tossed her one, then kicked his feet out in front of him. Weariness settled into his joints as if they had been waiting for him to get still. His hands ached with the wet and the long hours clutching the steering wheel, and his legs felt rubbery from slogging through the water. A chill squeezed his lungs as he remembered the last creek he'd forded. "Damn," he said aloud. "I really almost drowned out there."

"What happened?"

"Tree branch knocked my feet out from under me and I lost my bearings." He closed his eyes and leaned his head back against the wall. The pounding of the rain overhead filled the room.

Water in his mouth, his nose; his hair tangling in the branch . . .

He started, realizing he'd almost dozed off with all his earthly goods stuffed soaking wet inside his pack. Blinking, he pulled it over. "You mind if I spread some things out? It's all soaked and it'll mildew if I don't get it dry."

"Of course not."

There were jeans and socks and shirts. The underwear gave him a moment's pause, but the thought of doing without the next day or two made him spread it out along with everything else. A sack of oranges, a sodden box of cookies, several tins of Vienna sausages and a bottle of water followed. "This'll all come in handy," he commented.

Celia picked up the soggy cookies. "Too bad. Oreos are my favorite."

He grinned. "Mine, too. Can't go anywhere without 'em."

"Maybe they'll dry."

"They'll taste like catfish now—like the bottom of the river."

Celia laughed. Her smile was filled with the kind of teeth that had been professionally polished every six months on the button. Pretty, he thought, nudging an empty space in his own mouth with his tongue. Expensive, too. There had been no one to pay for things like dentists for Eric and his sister. At least he'd been able to get hers fixed before she'd started to lose them.

There was a conglomeration of other things in the pack—cards and dice for long nights or afternoons stranded in truck stops; scissors and soap; a saturated towel; string and hooks for makeshift fishing. Celia watched him sift through everything without saying anything, but when he pulled out the last item, he heard her make a noise. Not a gasp or a groan, but something in between.

"Something wrong?" he asked, holding the rubber-banded paperback in his hands. He glanced at it, and grinned as the truth came home. "Your dad, right?"

"Right." There was something less than enthusiastic in her voice. "Please tell me I'm not stuck up here for heaven knows how long with one of his groupies."

Eric laughed and then licked the spot on his lip when it started to bleed again. "Don't make me laugh. It hurts."

"If you regale me with stories about how my dear departed daddy changed the way you looked at things, I'll tell every joke I've ever heard."

Eric pressed the dishrag she'd given him to the cut. "I promise." He tossed the book aside with an inward chuckle. Jacob Moon *was* his favorite writer, and for a lot of reasons. Obviously, his daughter had heard all of them before.

She stood up and matter-of-factly spread a blanket over the mattress. "You can sleep now, if you want to. You look beat, and I'm a night owl, anyway."

Eric admired the rounded contours of her rear end briefly as she smoothed the blanket. His gaze fell with greater hunger to the pillow, however, and he nodded wearily. His mouth and hands hurt, his legs would barely hold him and he had driven so hard to get to Gideon that he'd had no sleep in thirty-six hours. "Much obliged," he said. As soon as his head sank into the downy recesses of a clean-smelling pillow, his brain spun away.

Along toward morning, there was a break in the rain. Celia had slept curled against the wall below the window, her head pillowed on the sill, her body wrapped in a blanket.

The cessation of noise was what startled her into wakefulness. No rain pounding overhead, no lightning and thunder flashing and roaring. She blinked, disoriented at first, then remembered the past eight hours. It was impossible to see much outside in the predawn darkness, although a little light pushed at the horizon. Another cloudy day, she thought with a groan.

Eric still slept, and even in the darkness she could see that it was the utterly unconscious sprawl of exhaustion. She crept past him quietly and tiptoed onto the landing just outside the attic door.

A silt-heavy smell of water hit her nostrils, and the air was heavy with moisture. If the sun came out any time soon, Celia thought fuzzily, they were in for scorching weather. She fumbled for the banister and found it, then headed down the stairs for the bathroom.

Beneath her bare feet, the wooden stairs were almost slimy with dampness. A shudder of unease whipped over her spine. A collection of unfamiliar noises began to penetrate the fog of awakening—a splash and trickle, a queer echoing. Below all that was a minute groaning, like the hull of a boat at sea.

She froze for an instant. Then, propelled by horrified curiosity, she continued down the steep flight of stairs, gripping the banister fiercely. Another splash sounded just as her toes hit icy cold water. Celia scrambled backward for an instant.

After a moment, she stepped back onto the submerged step, and holding with all her might to the banister with one hand, squatted and reached out with the other hand as far as she could. Water.

What had she expected? That somehow ankle-deep water had pooled on the twelfth step down?

A noise she couldn't identify sent her scurrying backward up the stairs, her heart pounding in her throat, her mind filled with thoughts of snakes: water moccasins, copperheads, cottonmouths—and whatever other kinds there were. It seemed as if she had learned the names of more evil snakes every day since her arrival in Texas. The noxious creatures were the one blemish on a landscape she otherwise loved.

Inside the attic room, she found an old tin bucket in a corner and carried it out to the landing, closing the door for privacy. For a moment, her nose filled with the river smell and her imagination with the triangular heads of snakes, she wondered if it might be easier to just hope Eric didn't awaken. Only the thought that he, too, would have to attend to the business of nature decided her. It was better than nothing—and a person couldn't go forever without using the bathroom, after all.

When she returned to the room, a gray dawn had begun to fill the long room, illuminating aging trunks shoved under the eaves. An old bicycle hung from the rafters, and a long oval mirror reflected the wan light. The boxes of supplies were clustered near the door.

In the middle of the wide room was the mattress they had dragged upstairs together, and upon it slept the man who had appeared so suddenly on her doorstep. Eric Putman, she thought, cocking her head. Last night, her impressions had been hurried, a little blurred, and she'd awakened with the feeling that she had dreamed him.

He slept on his back, a hand splayed on his chest, his long, long legs sprawled. He looked, she thought, as though he'd been knocked out in a fight and dragged, unconscious, to sleep it off.

His hair was every bit as black as it had looked the night before, and it was too long, curling around his muscled brown neck with abandon. His jaw was grizzled with black beard, and the painful-looking cut on his mouth made his already full lower lip swell.

My Lord in heaven, Celia thought. Her eyes crept over his thighs in the too-tight jeans that had belonged to her grandfather, slid over his lean hips and his broad-shouldered torso. Not a flaw. Not a single one.

She sighed softly, leaning against the wall, not quite sure whether to be thankful or distraught.

It was then that her gaze caught on his hands. They were as big as the rest of him, and just as lean—the kind of hands that gray-haired piano teachers exclaimed over in children—gracefully shaped and long fingered; strong and beautiful, like the man himself.

But the hands, unlike the man, were flawed. Thin ribbons of pale scar tissue criss-crossed the elegant lines of bone and marred the exquisite line of his fingers. One hand held the other in a loose grip, as if it had been aching while he slept.

A faraway rumble of thunder dragged her attention back to the here and now, and she crossed the room to peer out the window.

At the sight that greeted her, Celia felt another primeval shudder. The river ordinarily looped behind the farmhouse on a sleepy, muddy path to the Gulf. And on the far bank, Celia could see things were pretty much as they always had been—a meadow of thick grass met a stand of heavy trees. In the soft gray dawn, the scene shimmered with rain.

But on the farmhouse side, Jezebel had leapt her boundaries with hedonistic abandon. Thick-looking water swirling with tree branches and debris buried the cultivated lawn around the house. The oak and pecan trees around the house had been swallowed to the juncture of their branches and appeared to float eerily above the water.

And even as she watched, rain began to fall anew, pattering and plopping into the inland sea as if on a gentle springtime mission.

"Quite a sight," Eric commented behind her. The graveled sound of his voice purred over her spine and she turned with a little shock. The voice, too, had been real, she realized with a touch of wonder.

"It's terrifying," Celia said.

He glanced at the sky with eyes blue as a summer twilight, then to the waterlogged landscape beyond. He pursed his lips for a minute. "I don't think she's quite finished with her little temper tantrum, but I reckon we aren't gonna drown, either."

"I started to go downstairs," Celia commented, crossing her arms over her chest at the memory. "There's probably three or four feet of water down there. I wonder how it got in so badly."

"I opened the windows and doors," he said, and she felt him move away from her. "Otherwise, Jezebel would have just smashed her way in anyway."

"Oh." She felt daunted suddenly by all she didn't know. Gideon had seemed like a safe, dependable refuge from the insanity of her parents' constant, restless travel. In the space of twelve hours, that refuge had been snatched away.

Some of her dismay must have shown, because a big, heavy hand landed comfortingly on her shoulder. It rested there only an instant, but Celia felt the lack of its strength when Eric took it away. She turned suddenly. "You know, it scared me when you showed up last night," she said, "but I'm glad I'm not alone in this."

A slow, lazy smile spread over his dark face. "Careful, sugar."

Her own mouth quirked in a wry smile. "I have an instinct about these things," she returned. "I had to." She stuck her hands into her back pocket and cleared her throat. "I—uh—rigged up a sort of latrine or whatever you want to call it out there on the landing."

His grin broadened. "Something tells me you would have been just fine by yourself up here."

"I didn't mean to imply I needed help," she said. "Just that it's easier not to have to face it alone."

"Okay." He gathered up a few belongings from the floor and ducked out to the landing. The door snicked closed behind him.

A rumble sounded in her belly and Celia knelt by the boxes of food. She'd kill for a cup of coffee right now. It was such a deeply ingrained part of her morning routine that she didn't know how she would shake the fuzziness it usually cleared.

The lack of coffee made the rest of the provisions look utterly unappealing. Peanut butter for breakfast? Nope. Vienna sausages? Forget it. Finally she found what she sought: a box of strawberry toaster pastries with sprinkle frosting. She settled on the bed with the box in one hand, an orange in the other and forced herself to stop dreaming of caffeine.

Eric returned in a few minutes. His hair was combed, and he'd changed from her grandfather's clothes into some of his own—a red flannel shirt with the sleeves rolled to the elbows and very old jeans, soft as the flannel in his shirt, worn colorless. And obviously, Celia thought with a jolt, they had always been his jeans. They cupped and caressed and clung in ways that might have been indecent if—

The orange she'd been peeling squirted juice in her eye as if in punishment for her lascivious thoughts. Annoyed, she squeezed it closed. Jeans were just jeans, she told herself. It wasn't as though he'd suddenly appeared in his underwear.

She risked another peek and decided he might as well have.

A can of cola landed with a heavy thud near her ankle. "Where did this come from?" she asked, popping the can open.

"Same place I got everything else."

"Thank God," she murmured, and drank greedily. "I can't think without caffeine."

"You'd get used to it if you had to." He stood near the window, staring pensively at the gray beyond. Celia thought it was worry that crossed his features.

"Is something wrong?"

He shrugged. "I hope not." He drank a long swallow of cola. "My sister's out there, somewhere. That's how I got stuck last night. Kept thinking if I could just keep moving, I'd make it to her place." His jaw hardened for an instant, then he flashed Celia a smile over his shoulder. "Problem is, I'd have had to cross Jezebel, and I don't think she was in the mood last night."

"I think you're right." Celia offered the box of pastries and Eric settled on the edge of the bed, taking one.

"How's your lip this morning?" she asked, eyeing the angry cut.

"I'll live."

"Can I tell you my jokes yet?"

One side of his mouth lifted. "Not unless you want me to start telling you how your daddy changed my perspective."

"No, thanks." Celia put the last of the pastry into her mouth and brushed her palms clean. "I've had enough of that to last me for the rest of my life."

Eric nodded and light danced in his thick black hair, swirling over his crown like the water outside. "I bet it was hard to be Jacob Moon's daughter."

"By himself, he would have been okay, but I was also Dahlia Larsen's daughter." She rolled her eyes. "Between the two of them, we never went out in public without a camera flashing."

"With parents like that, you must be pretty talented yourself."

It was the typical response and Celia was oddly disappointed. "No, afraid not." She stacked orange peelings in a small pile. "I can write a passable sonnet in three languages, dance tap, ballet and jazz without killing myself and accompany any church choir in the world on piano."

"Sounds like a lot to me."

"I had a great education," she said. "I just don't have a drop of talent." She smiled at this admission, attempting to hold off the sympathetic noises people usually made at this point.

Instead, Eric plucked an orange slice from the ball in his hand and chewed it slowly. "Did you ever want to do any of those things?"

"No, not at all. I studied hard, of course, because my parents expected it, but I never enjoyed them."

"That's why then. You've got to love something to make it work."

"I love teaching," she said. "I'm really good at it, too."

For some reason, this brought a grin to his face. "Miss Moon?" he teased. "I bet the kids go crazy."

"Yes. Always. Doesn't usually last long, though."

"What do you teach? English?"

"Heaven forbid." She shuddered for effect. "I teach high school math." She loved telling people this, loved watching their perception of her undergo the change it always did. No one expected a wispy little blonde to be teaching algebra and calculus.

Eric didn't disappoint her. "Really?" he said, and his chin jutted out a little as he looked at her for a long moment. "You mean algebra and all that?"

She smiled. "Yes."

"And you love it." His tone was disbelieving.

Her smile broadened. "Yes."

"How can anybody love algebra?" he asked, then held up a hand. "Sorry, that's rude."

Celia laughed. "No, it's normal. Most people are terrified of numbers and think they're governed by some obscure set of rules and regulations only a genius can understand." She leaned forward, resting her elbows on her knees. "But even when I was little, I loved fractions and equations. I badgered my father for a month to teach me how to carry and borrow when I was six."

"But *why* do you love all those equations?"

His question seemed more intensely focused than the ones she usually heard. "Why?" Celia echoed. "I don't know." She looked toward the grayness beyond the window, trying to find words for an abstract idea. The picture that came to mind when she thought about math was one of an ordered row of prisms, row upon row of them, stretching into infinity. "They're so orderly," she said.

"I'll tell you," he said. "I never could conquer algebra. It drove me crazy. No matter what angle I came at it from, I couldn't make it work, couldn't see how to make it clear in my mind." He shook his head slowly. "I really admire people who can."

She heard in his voice not the muddled who-cares-anyway attitude of many people regarding math, but the genuine frustration of one who had tried and couldn't breach the language. "You probably had a teacher who made assumptions about how people learn that weren't right for you, or—" she grinned "—you're hopelessly right brained."

His heavy, dark eyebrows raised. "Had a good teacher, so you fill in the blanks."

"Right brained." Her heart sunk a little. Right brained meant creative, which meant like her parents, which meant this man was poison. "What do you do?"

He'd been open and fluent until that moment. Now his face shuttered with an almost audible slam of defensive armor. "Nothing," he said, and stood up. "I don't do anything."

Celia looked at his hands braced on the windowsill as he glared at the rain. His unspoken words echoed into the room as loudly and clearly as if he'd shouted them.

Not anymore.

Chapter Three

Eric thought if it rained one more hour, he would go crazy. All day, it had continued. Pattering, dripping, smacking, trickling. The incessant sound wore on him like torture.

To make matters worse, the air in the attic room grew stale with their breathing and a stifling humidity. In spite of the storm, it wasn't exactly cool, either, and Eric knew from experience what they'd be in for when the rain stopped and the flood abated: jungle weather.

Restlessly, he prowled the perimeters of the room, pacing between the trunks at one end to the boxes and discards at the other, tapping the windowsill with his hand as he passed, flipping the doorknob on the other side of the room as he passed it.

Celia stretched out on the mattress, reading a thick novel she'd brought upstairs with her last night. She was only halfway through it and had been reading most of the day, and she kept reading now in spite of his pacing.

Part of his problem was the picture she made in that soft bed, her long, slender legs stretched out, her hip jutting up casually, a spray of silvery hair spilling over the hand that propped her up. Sometimes she flipped over onto her tummy and he had to contend with the high, round contours of her fanny—one of the prettiest rear ends he'd yet had the pleasure of admiring.

It was clear that she was not the sort of woman who wore her beauty with knowledge and an edge of manipulation. He doubted she even knew that she was a beauty. He might have questioned the intelligence of a woman who had looked in the mirror at her face and body for twenty-plus years without coming to the obvious conclusion, but in this case, he was pretty sure he knew why. He'd seen pictures of her mother, the dancer. Dahlia had been full of breast and hip, with wide, exotic eyes that drove men wild. Her coloring had been vivid, her style polished.

Eric tapped the doorknob on his way by, his fingertips registering the pattern carved into brass. He had known women like Dahlia, driven by a need for recognition from everyone. Retta, with her wild beauty, came to mind.

Eric frowned and pushed the thought away, deliberately calling forth a picture of Celia's mother. He'd seen too often how women like her had operated, and

Celia had probably faded into the background a lot more than was good for a little girl.

He glanced at her, sprawled unselfconsciously on the bed, the swell of one breast peeking demurely over the edge of her scoop-necked shirt. Instantly, he felt a restless pulse below his belt.

Dog, he told himself, forcing his gaze back toward the window where rain splatted and patted and smacked against the glass. She wasn't his kind of woman. There was a fragility and honor about her that was so far removed from the lusty women he'd known on the road that it was hard to imagine they were the same species. And the truth was, he liked his women ripe, even a little bawdy. It saved time.

No, he corrected himself. That made those women sound cheap, and they weren't. They were just like him—raised to fend for themselves, to fight for whatever they got. When you had to scramble for your daily bread, it put the niceties of social convention into perspective—life was too hard and too short to waste on ridiculous social dances, particularly if both parties knew ahead of time what they were looking for.

He tapped the windowsill on another restless round. No, Celia Moon was not his type. She'd need some wooing, and once bedded, she'd expect more than he'd ever be able to give.

Why, then, had he spent the day half-aroused?

At the window he paused, noting the water level was still rising, although it had slowed somewhat. On impulse, he threw the casement open and inhaled deeply the cooler, fresher air that sailed through.

From behind him, Celia spoke, her voice amused. "Too bad you can't dive from there and go swimming. It would probably make you feel better."

He glanced over his shoulder and felt himself grin. "Doesn't it drive you crazy, being trapped like this?"

"A little." She put the book down, face first. "I learned early how to amuse myself almost anywhere, so it's not so bad, really."

With a nimble movement, she stood up and stretched. For one weak moment Eric admired the narrowness of her waist, the long lines of her arms and legs, then shifted his gaze. "I hate the sound of it. It grates on my nerves. Pat, pat, pat, pat—"

She laughed. "I was thinking exactly the same thing last night before you showed up. I made popcorn so that I wouldn't have to listen to it." She dug into the boxes of provisions and came up with a can of Vienna sausages, a sleeve of crackers and peanut butter. "Want something to eat?"

Eric wanted to growl at her, wanted to tell her he could think of better ways to forget about the storm. He had an appetite for something besides eating. But it wasn't her fault she made him hungry or that she wasn't the kind of woman to ease that hunger without some return. "Sure," he said, exhaling suddenly, and pointed to the window. "You mind if I leave this open? There's not much rain coming in."

"Considering everything," she said, "a little rain on the floor of the attic isn't going to bother me much."

After they ate, Celia dragged one of the trunks away from the corner, brushing cobwebs from it. Eric settled on the edge of the mattress and pulled out his harmonica to fiddle with while he watched. "What's in there?" he asked.

"I don't know. Thought it might be fun to see."

The latch had an old key still dangling from it, and it turned easily. "I hope it's not filled with black widows," Celia said with a wrinkled nose.

"They're more afraid of you than you are of them."

Her wide, pale eyes reflected utter skepticism. "I seriously doubt that." She stood up, gripped the edge of the trunk lid and took a long, deep breath. She flung it open, then jumped back.

Eric chuckled over her peering into the trunk from three feet back. She inched closer, her chin jutting out as she stretched her neck to make sure there were no spiders inside.

He couldn't resist. Just as she reached the trunk, assuring herself there were no creepy crawlies inside, he jumped forward. "Boo."

Celia flinched, then her eyes narrowed. "That was mean."

"A little," Eric agreed cheerfully, and blew a quick scurry of notes through his harmonica.

"You're not afraid of anything, I suppose?"

"I'm afraid of the dark." He looked at her. "And airplanes and floods."

"Airplanes? Why?"

He shrugged. "Why are you afraid of spiders?"

"Because they can get under your clothes and in your hair and bite you."

"Well, I hate the idea of being fifty thousand feet in the air with only five feet of steel between me and the ground. It makes me sick to my stomach."

"Do you fly anyway?"

"Only when there's no other way." He grinned. "And I drink a lot of Jack Daniel's."

She bent her head over the trunk and pulled out a crocheted baby blanket, then a pair of tiny leather shoes. "These must have been my dad's," she said. A flicker of anger crossed her face, but in contrast, her fingers stroked the blanket reverently. With a tightness around her lips, she put the articles aside and dug deeper, pulling out more baby clothes and then a christening outfit. "Oh, my," she exclaimed. "This is incredible." She held it out to Eric. "Feel that satin."

Obligingly, he ran the back of his hand over it, and was surprised at the luxurious coolness of it. "Nice."

"Do people still get babies christened?"

"Around here they sure do. This is the Bible Belt, sister. Folks take saving souls very seriously." For emphasis, he began to play a mournful "Amazing Grace." He started with the intention of amusing her, but the old spiritual seduced him, pulling him deeper into itself, and he found his attention slipping away. There was a little turn he'd never played before, and he drew it out, closing his eyes to hear it more thoroughly.

Abruptly he remembered where he was and stopped. Celia sat before the open trunk, staring at him, her hands wrapped around the christening outfit. "That was beautiful," she said softly. "Why did you quit?"

He saw something in the big, silvery eyes that puzzled him, an expression of disappointment mixed with wonder. It reminded him of the anger and tenderness with which she had regarded her father's baby blanket. Curious suddenly, he asked, "Where's your daddy now?"

"Heaven or hell, whichever Saint Peter decided upon when he reached the gates." She didn't look at Eric, but dipped again into the trunk to pull out a stack of old-fashioned school record books.

"He's dead?" Eric asked without thinking how tactless it sounded until after the words were out of his mouth. As usual.

Celia took a breath. "Both of them are. My mother died about eighteen months ago, very suddenly of an embolism." She cleared her throat. "My father had a car accident about three months later."

The way she said "accident" made it sound like the exact opposite. Eric didn't say anything for a minute. What was there to say?

When the silence stretched, Celia put the notebooks aside and continued with her treasure hunt. A frown touched her face as she withdrew a bundle wrapped in heavy plastic, taped and sealed. Without warning, she tossed it to Eric. He caught it, but just barely. The box was heavy and solid.

"You got a mean side yourself, don't you?"

"If that's what I think it is, it's only fitting you should open it." She dragged another one out and dropped it with a thunk to the floor beside him.

Eric stroked the box, feeling the satiny dust of years on the plastic covered cardboard. Nothing else had the heft of a pile of pages. These were manuscripts.

A sharp prick of excitement clutched his chest, and for an instant, it scared him. It had been so long since he'd felt anything. With a distinct sense of surprise, he noticed his hands were trembling slightly as he un-taped the plastic around the heavy white box and lifted the lid.

When he read the neatly typed title page, his stom-ach leapt wildly, once. "*Song of Mourning*," it read, "by Jacob Moon." His first novel, published in the late fifties to critical acclaim and popular success.

Eric looked at the slight, silver-haired woman who stood watching him with impassive features. "Ce-lia," he said, and he heard the wonder in his voice. "You...this...I can't—" Words failed and he shook his head.

"Now you have something to do," she said quietly. A note of something almost tender permeated her voice, and he looked up in surprise. She smiled, her arms crossed over her chest, and for a moment she again didn't seem quite real. Her beauty was ethereal, not quite of this plane, and he had the strangest feel-ing that she had delivered some message and would now disappear.

Come to think of it, did Jacob Moon even have a daughter?

Disoriented, Eric jumped up, urgently reaching out a hand to touch her arm. To his relief—and embar-rassment—it was warm, slender but sturdy, and defi-nitely mortal.

Her smile widened into a grin and without warn-ing, she touched his cheek. He felt her fingers rasp over the bristles of his beard and then fall away. "En-joy yourself," she said.

She crossed the room and tugged out another trunk, and Eric watched her for a puzzled moment, utterly confused. Had he just snapped at long last?

Outside the rain picked up tempo, beginning once again to pour in heavy bucketfuls to the already saturated earth. Eric clenched his teeth against a ripple of dread and turned his attention to the other manuscripts.

Each was bundled in exactly the same fashion—packed first in a white box, then wrapped in heavy plastic. In the days before computers, he supposed, it had been important to have backup copies of a manuscript in a safe place. Jacob Moon had obviously sent a copy of each of his books to his mother's house for safekeeping.

Eric had read all of the books at one time or another, but it gave him chills to hold the actual manuscripts in his hands. He'd told Celia jokingly that he wouldn't talk about her father, and he would stick to that. But he wished, suddenly, that he could share some of his thoughts.

Because, the truth was, he didn't just like the novels of this man. They had been his anchors through the hard years after he'd left home, a way to hang on to the smells and sounds and even the people of Gideon, a place he loved and hated in equal portions.

Much as Jacob Moon did. Jacob, too, had run from this little hellhole of a town, run when he was young, just as Eric had done. But every book he'd ever written was set in a mythical town everybody knew was Gideon.

He looked at Celia, who had wrapped a lacy, long-fringed shawl around her shoulders. Her hair was caught under the edges and as he watched, she shook out a soft black dress. Even from across the room, he could see her eyes light up.

What was her story? he wondered now. What had drawn her back to her father's roots, to a town in the middle of nowhere she'd never lived in? What was she looking for?

With a shock, he heard the deep curiosity in his thoughts and combined with the sharp hunger he'd felt a little while ago, that was a bad sign. Mind your own business, he told himself.

A woman like Celia could only bring trouble. Lord knew he'd already had his share. Setting his jaw in determination, he turned his attention to the manuscripts and lost himself in another world, a world that didn't have at its center a compelling woman he could never possess.

By nightfall the water level had risen again. Celia crept down the stairs to check, gritting her teeth against the thought of snakes as she counted steps. This morning, the twelfth step down had been covered with water. Now the eleventh had disappeared, as well. The candle flame flickered over the narrow sea trapped in the stairwell, dancing like a lantern on a ship's prow over the ocean.

From the top of the stairs, Eric spoke. "Come on back up here, sugar. There's nothing you can do."

For a moment, she paused, thinking of all the things buried now below the ravaging river. "She's ruined all my grandma's things," Celia said and looked over her shoulder at him. "Jezebel has ruined it all."

"Come on back upstairs, Celia," he repeated, holding out one big hand toward her. "You'll just make yourself sick thinking of it."

His voice was gentle and persuasive. Celia climbed the stairs and took his hand. His palm was smooth and hard, and his fingers engulfed hers. Despite the tangled ribbons of scars on his flesh, there was a strength that seemed to promise comfort.

She looked up to his face and found him watching her with an oddly understanding expression as she climbed up to stand beside him.

"Are we doing to die?" Celia asked.

He hesitated, then lifted his free hand to brush a strand of hair from her face. "No," he said finally, the word a bass rumble in his raw, dark voice.

Celia didn't care if it was a lie. All at once, she didn't care about anything except the puzzling gift of him standing there in front of her with his lonely eyes and beautiful face and seductive voice.

With a sudden ferocity that shocked her, Celia wanted to kiss him. She wanted to taste the full shape of his mouth against her tongue, to feel the prickles of his beard against her chin; wanted to feel his strong arms envelop her.

And for an instant, she thought she might. His body swayed infinitesimally closer; his eyes darkened and swept over her mouth.

Then he abruptly straightened and let go of her hand. "You're some kind of woman," he said, then turned and went into the room.

Celia followed, carrying the candle, a strange tingling running through her body. Eric dropped to the floor beside the window, plucking his harmonica from his pocket to draw a few restless notes through it in much the same way another man might use a cigarette.

Celia took a breath and settled on the bed. What had just happened? Was it her wishful imagination or had he almost kissed her? And if so, what had made him stop? She certainly wouldn't have resisted.

But there would be no answers from him, even if she'd known how to phrase them delicately. He had closed himself off visibly, erecting the barrier she'd come to recognize over the past twenty-four hours—an abrupt, thorough withdrawal that fairly bristled.

She picked up her novel, but realized she was sick of reading and digging through trunks and eating. The flood had passed from an exciting phenomenon to a terrifying one in just a few hours. She was scared.

Ignoring the warning signs of Eric's retreat, Celia spoke. "I always wanted to come to Gideon," she began. "It seemed like everything safe and normal was here—my grandma and people who'd lived in one place all their lives and knew each other since kindergarten."

Eric looked at her but didn't speak. It was encouragement enough. "When we visited, I loved to listen to my grandma's stories—she knew the history of everyone in town. It amazed me. We never stayed anywhere longer than a year."

"So now you're here," he said. "Not so safe, after all, is it?"

Celia frowned. The flood hadn't really changed anything in her heart, she realized. "Yes, it is. And maybe it wasn't safety I was looking for as much as stability."

He grinned, a devastating, devilish half grin that put a teasing light into his dark blue eyes. "Come on, Celia, admit it—you came here looking for the place your daddy loved so much."

"Loved?" Celia echoed with narrowed eyes. "No. He *loved* his books and he *loved* my mother." She folded her hands neatly in her lap. "Sometimes, if he wasn't too busy with those other things, he loved me. But I think he hated Texas. If he'd loved it, he would have let me stay here and grow up like a normal person. I begged him often enough."

Eric opened the bottle of Jack Daniel's he had carried in his backpack and poured a little into two paper cups. "Go ahead," he rasped when Celia shook her head. "It'll make you feel better."

Celia accepted the offering and tasted it experimentally. The heat she expected, but not the sweet, smoky undernotes. She looked at it in surprise. "It's good," she said, and took another sip.

For some reason, her reaction pleased him. The look on his face was reluctantly admiring. "Thought you didn't like whiskey."

"My mother drank Scotch." She rolled her eyes. "*Lots* of Scotch. I thought all whiskey was the same."

"Nope." He poured a little more into each of their glasses and replaced the cap. "I don't know what exactly drove your daddy away from here, Celia, but he loved Gideon." He gestured toward the neat pile of original manuscripts near the bed. "Every word he wrote, he wrote about this place. And he wrote about it the way a man writes about a lover—he understood everything about it, every little nuance."

"I thought we weren't going to talk about him," Celia said, sipping again. A calm warmth spread over her spine, welcome and relaxing.

"You started it, sugar." He grinned, then winced and touched the cut on his lip. "I kinda got the impression you wanted to talk."

She had. She did. All afternoon she had watched him surreptitiously as he reverently leafed through her father's manuscripts. "You really love his books, don't you?"

"When I left home," Eric said slowly, "there were some very hard years when I had to learn how to get along with the world. It wasn't easy." He took a breath and paused so long, Celia thought he wouldn't go on. He didn't tell this story often. "Whenever I got so homesick I was ready to pack it in, I'd just read one of his books again and I'd feel okay. Until the next time."

"But what makes it sound like Gideon to you?" she asked. "I keep looking and I haven't found the Gideon he was writing about."

With a secretive smile, Eric picked up his harmonica and began to play. The notes were slow and rich and made her think of the river winding through town on a late summer afternoon. As Eric played—and it was playful, not serious—she could see thick, yellow sunshine pouring through cattails and gnats hanging in whirling clouds above the lazy water, and she could taste sweet tea and mint on her tongue.

When he put the harmonica down and sipped his whiskey, she said, "How do you do that?"

"Do what?"

"Make me see pictures when you play that thing." She frowned at him. "I've heard 'Amazing Grace' a thousand times and I never saw pictures in my mind before this afternoon."

His amusement increased. "What did you see, Celia?"

She recalled the picture in perfect clarity—a simple clapboard church, painted white, with a congregation assembled outside it, a sunny Sunday morning. "Never mind," she said more sharply than she intended.

Eric laughed. The sound was as rough and deep and dark as his voice. It rumbled in the air and settled in Celia's shoulders, then ran softly through her body. As if he'd touched her with seductive fingers, she felt quivers in her breasts and in the small of her back and along the backs of her thighs.

She put her glass down precisely. "I'd like a little more, please."

Eric obliged her. "It's the blues," he said.

"What?"

Carefully, he added a short measure to his own glass before he replied. "It's the blues that makes you see those pictures in your head. Some people do, some people don't. But you're one of the ones that does. So was your daddy. That's what's in his books, that same feeling."

The blues. She measured him for a moment. "Are you a musician?" A part of her prayed he would say no. Another part prayed the answer was yes, because then she could free herself from this ridiculous attraction to him.

His eyes shuttered. "I told you already," he said. "I don't do anything."

"You must do something," she said.

"Nope." He leaned back against the wall. "Just keep moving."

The walls had slammed into place again. Celia wondered if the answer that he was a drifter was better or worse than the one she'd been dreading.

Then all at once, she saw the situation for what it was—a handsome drifter and a lone woman trapped together in a Texas flood. It was a scenario straight out of one of her father's novels.

The realization infuriated her, and she turned her back suddenly on Eric with his mysterious life and marred hands and ability to make her see pictures. A woman in her father's books would be helpless and hungry.

A woman in one of his novels would wonder who the drifter was and want to heal his wounds. Somehow the pair would find a bittersweet love—and then, somehow, tragedy would separate them, leaving the pair wandering alone and disconnected forever.

Well, she'd see her father in hell before she'd play one of his characters for the satisfaction of absurd Fate.

She closed her eyes tight. Forget it, she thought. Just forget it.

Chapter Four

In his dreams, his hands were whole and strong. He could see them as he curled around the body of his guitar, his fingers straight, the tips callused from the strings. In his dreams, there were no scars riddling the flesh and there was deftness in their speed.

In his dreams, his hands were beautiful with power.

But when he woke, his left was clasped in his right, each trying to ease the ache of the other. He didn't have to move his fingers to know how stiff they would be.

A small moan of frustration and sorrow escaped his mouth before he knew it was coming, and he leaned his head back against the wall in the darkness. Why did he keep dreaming of perfect hands? He might have borne nightmares of the accident or it's aftermath—

might even have expected them. He might have understood his guilt-ridden soul torturing him with the visions of Retta or the sound of her screams.

Instead, his mind cast out cruel visions of his hands, whole and perfect. Each time he awakened from the dream, he believed for an instant it was true. Each morning he lost his hands anew.

Celia's voice, slumberous and soft, came to him through the gloom. "Eric?"

He didn't answer, hoping she would believe him asleep.

"Eric?" she called again.

"I'm all right, Celia. Go on back to sleep."

"You can't be comfortable over there. Come lie down. There's room for both of us."

At another time, a time when the darkness was not so thick, a time when he'd not just learned for the six hundredth time that his hands were broken beyond repair, he might have resisted. Even as he stood up and crossed the room, he told himself it was crazy. He was crazy.

He settled stiffly beside her, still holding his hands close to his body, where the warmth might ease the ache. A scent of patchouli and rose wafted over him, a strangely exotic scent for such a practical woman.

Her hands, small and a little cold, surprised him. They settled over his aching fingers with gentle, firm intent. "I've been awake for a while," she said. "Your hands hurt, don't they?"

Without waiting for a reply, she lifted one into her palm and with the other hand began to massage the aching joints with purposeful, honest pressure. "My dad had terrible arthritis in his hands the past six or eight years. He said it was from typing so much of his life.''

Eric groaned softly at the release of stiffness and pain her fingers wrought. He didn't question the source of relief. He settled back on the pillows, feeling tension slide away from his shoulders and neck as her quiet soothing voice rambled on like a lullaby.

''You must have arthritis, too,'' she continued softly. ''You're so young, you'll have to make sure you exercise them every day or you won't be able to use them at all.''

She let go of his left hand and picked up his right. But when she started to talk again, he reached through the darkness to touch her mouth. Her hands stilled for an instant, along with her words.

He'd meant only to stop the flow of commentary, stop it as gently as he knew how. But his fingers registered the plumpness of her lower lip and he found himself exploring the curve, feeling her breath sough moistly over his fingertips. He traced the bow on the upper lip and the luscious swell of the lower, moved slowly from corner to corner.

She caught his palm and pulled away, but not before he imagined exploring the same path with his tongue.

''Eric,'' she whispered, half in protest, half in longing.

It was the longing that aroused him to an almost uncomfortable point—and also made him draw away. ''I'm sorry, Celia.''

She caught his arm as he rolled away from her. "You won't get any sleep on the floor." She eased away from him and tugged a blanket over her shoulders, turning her back as she nestled into the pillows. All he could see was her slight, feminine form and a fall of ice-colored hair.

He lifted a hand to reach for her, hungry all at once for the warmth of another person cradled against him, a warmth he'd not known in a long time. He wanted to tuck her close, wrap himself around her and go to sleep.

Instead, he grabbed an extra pillow and pressed it against the hollowness in his chest, knowing—even if she didn't—that he was not the kind of man she ought to be messing with.

Celia awakened to silence. No rain. For a long, long moment, she simply listened. And from beneath the silence, another sound penetrated her fuzzy morning brain. She opened her eyes, as if seeing could help her hear more clearly. Finally, she placed the sound.

Birdsong. There were birds out there! She turned toward the window in excitement.

It was only then that she became aware of the strange array of soft weights surrounding her. One pressed against her shoulder, another, her hip. Yet another anchored her ankles.

Slowly she shifted. Eric's forehead was pressed into her shoulder and she felt the silkiness of his curls against her neck. In sleep, his face lost its expression of wariness and the lines around his mouth eased, making him look very young and vulnerable.

The warmth upon her hip was his hand, and across her ankles was one bare foot.

She didn't move. It was as if he'd gravitated toward her as he slept, tentatively reaching for comfort without demanding anything in return. The thought made her heart constrict oddly, even more than the butterfly brush of his fingers on her lips last night.

Who was he? Behind the mask of toughness, beyond his gravelly, hard voice, who was the man inside? She touched his hand lightly, tracing a slender scar over the rise of tendons and bones. Such a big hand. The spread of his fingers covered her from the bend of her waist to the top of her thigh.

Last night his groan had pierced her. It had carried an edge of anguish and loss, like the cry of a wolf standing helpless over a wounded mate.

Who are you? she thought again.

Tiny stirrings in his arms and across his foot told her he was edging toward awakening. She closed her eyes, instinctively aware that when he discovered himself curled around her, he would feel exposed.

But he didn't immediately awaken. A low sound of contentment escaped his mouth and he moved closer, his hand circling her waist. Comfortably, he rubbed her stomach and threw a leg over her thighs.

Celia froze. He burrowed his face into the curve of her neck, stroking her shoulder with his rough-bristled chin. She could feel his forehead against her jaw and the tiny brush of his eyelashes a little lower. She held her breath.

As his fingers roved in a lazy, open-palmed circle over her torso, tiny buds of curiosity and desire grew plump on the stems of her nerves. She wondered what would happen if she shifted ever so slightly into his arms, wondered how it would feel to have his big body over hers, wondered what taste his lips would carry.

But what if he awakened?

Closing her eyes tight, she shifted as if in sleep, turning her back to him, hoping he *would* awaken and think her still lost in her own slumber.

Instead, he dropped his arm closer around her, tugging her firmly into the curl of his hard, long body. A mercurial wash of hunger burst through her veins. His forearm crossed her breasts and his hand cupped her shoulder.

The quicksilver desire expanded. Her breath seemed an airy, lost thing, unnecessary in the quiet morning with the heat of Eric surrounding her, enveloping her. Against her fanny, she felt his hard and unmistakable arousal and she clenched her teeth to control her instinctive need to move against it.

For an endless time she lay in his arms, afraid to move for fear he was soon to awaken, yet afraid not to for fear she would explode with the hunger he'd kindled so innocently. It shamed her oddly to feel the rigidness of her nipples against the loose clasp of his arm, and she knew he'd awaken and feel it and know....

His hand moved as if in time with her thoughts. His fingers slipped over her shoulder and traced the line of her collarbone and neck. Her heart thudded as he stroked the flesh above her blouse, then moved inexorably over the swell of her breast to that shamefully rigid peak. Her breath ceased as he expertly teased the sensitive flesh, and then gently settled his huge, broad palm over her breast, cupping her as if to gauge the fit of one to the other. Judging by the exquisite kneading of his fingers, it was a fit that pleased him.

Celia could stand no more. "Eric," she protested, her voice strangled and almost unrecognizable.

"I'm not asleep," he said, and his mouth opened on her neck, hot and fierce.

A shock of sensation rocketed over her again. His tongue, silky and warm, lashed her neck and Celia made a half-strangled noise of arousal and protest.

From a dozen points in her body, a whirl of explosions went up. His hair splayed over her jaw, cool and silky in contrast to the heat of his mouth on her neck. His fingers plucked expertly at her breast, and against her fanny, he pressed his rigid erection. His thigh moved restlessly over hers.

"I felt you wake up," he said in his raw voice. "You didn't get up. You just stayed here and let me touch you." He moved closer and sucked her earlobe into his mouth. "Don't you know any better than to tempt a hungry man, Celia?"

His voice. So dark and ragged and raw. His voice alone made her want to turn and push him down and turn his taunts to her advantage. She wanted to straddle him and disrobe and torment him the way he was tormenting her.

The lustiness of her thoughts stunned her. Miss Celia Moon, teacher of algebra and calculus, mild mannered and disgustingly practical, wanted to *straddle* this rough-edged stranger?

She grabbed his hand in panic and ducked her head away from his questing mouth. "Stop, Eric," she said, a catch in her voice.

Instantly he released her. One moment she was wrapped with him in a heated tangle. The next, she was alone and cold on the bed. She lay there for a minute, flushed with embarrassment and aching with the imprint of his hands.

There was no place for him to go. After a moment, Celia turned to look at him, standing by the open window, his arms braced on the sill, head bent against the pale light of morning. His hair was impossibly black, alluringly tousled. She followed the line of his muscled shoulders down his back, over the firm, delectable curve of his rear end, down his long, long legs.

The whistle of a magpie sailed in through the window and Celia jumped up. "It really has stopped raining!" she cried. The clouds overhead were thin, even growing wispy in places. A sense of jubilation rose in her chest. "Thank God."

As if on cue, the magpie she'd heard swooped close by the window, a twig with battered leaves in its mouth. Celia laughed. "Everything that happens around here has biblical overtones," she said, delighted.

He said nothing, and she turned. His dark blue eyes were bleak, his mouth set in hard lines. She touched his chest. "What is it?"

Jaw drawn tight, Eric shook his head, and for a moment, Celia thought he was going to erect his walls of protection. Then he looked at her and before the opaqueness could hide it, she saw the loneliness in his eyes, a yearning of such intensity it nearly broke her heart.

This time, she didn't wait for him, nor did she care that her father would write this scene in just this way.

She stepped forward and wrapped her arms around his broad body, pressing her face into the soft flannel over his chest. After an instant of hesitation, his arms dropped around her, but lightly, loosely, as if he were afraid to accept what she offered.

A dozen things ran through her mind as she hugged him. Things she should say, like *everything is going to be all right*. Things she should do, like rock him back and forth in the ancient rhythm of comfort.

Instead she just stood there, still and calm, letting him absorb the warmth of her body, the warmth he'd so tentatively sought as he'd slept and couldn't accept when he awakened.

He was the loneliest man she'd ever met. She didn't know how she knew that or why he'd come to this point. It didn't matter.

She held him. For now, for this moment, it was enough.

As the hours of the morning passed, it was plain the storm had passed. The sky cleared of even wispy clouds, and the floodwaters began to recede with almost astonishing speed.

After a few moments of silence and awkwardness, Eric and Celia ate a breakfast of the last toaster pastries washed down with tepid water. Then, as if by common agreement, they each retreated to separate corners. Eric played his harmonica restlessly. Celia pretended to read her book.

Toward noon, the attic began to heat up as the strong Texas sun beat down upon the shingles of the roof. Eric got out a deck of cards. "Come on," he said as Celia poked through the provisions with a frown. "Play a hand or two of gin rummy while you eat and you won't care so much about what you're putting in your belly."

She nodded at this peace offering and settled across from him to play cards.

But as the afternoon passed, the temperature climbed inexorably. Restlessly, Celia stood up to check the progress of the water. "How long do you think it'll take until the water goes?"

"By morning we'll be able to get out of here, I imagine." Celia heard him reshuffle the cards. "You anxious to get rid of me?"

She heard the teasing note in his words and glanced over her shoulder ruefully, shoving wisps of hair from her face. "Yesterday you were the restless one. Today it's me." She leaned out the window. "I guess I just want to get out in the sunshine. Seems like it's been raining for a year."

Eric stretched out on the wooden floor and flipped the queen of spades over the king of hearts in his solitaire game. "We'll see how you feel about that pretty sunshine by tomorrow noon."

She shrugged. "I don't mind the heat. It's cold I can't stand."

"You ever spend a summer here?"

"Once, a long time ago."

He flipped the jack of diamonds over the queen, then looked at Celia with a gleam in his dark blue eyes. "Bet you won't like heat much by the time you get through this summer."

She frowned. "You don't know that. Maybe I'm naturally thin blooded and the cold makes me miserable."

"Maybe." He raised an eyebrow. "Maybe you just don't know about real heat." As if his words had reminded him, he stood up and started to unbutton his flannel shirt.

When he reached for a T-shirt folded on top of his pack, Celia glanced out toward the meadow across the water. She could do without the sight of his exposed torso, thank you very much. "Is everyone in Texas a know-it-all?" she asked.

His ragged chuckle almost—but not quite—tempted her to turn around. "Don't you know there's not a Texan born who doesn't know everything? 'Course, we all know a little bit of something nobody else knows."

She pivoted, unable to stop herself. He tugged the flannel shirt from his arms, pulling the sleeves inside out, and discarded it on the bed. Absently, he touched his chest in the way men will do, as if to ascertain all the ribs were still in place. It was a gesture Celia had seen a hundred times, but as his scarred hand moved over his taut stomach and broad torso, the hunger of the morning returned full force.

She swallowed against the wash of desire, fighting it, yet staring as if bewitched. It was not just that he was so big and well proportioned or that his body spoke of time spent outside with a hammer or a hoe. It was not even the casual intimacy and comfort with which he touched himself.

It was his skin—sleek and supple, tanned to a soft copper. Every inch of his flesh gleamed with a satiny sheen. Not a single hair marred the perfection. His hand slid away from his chest, and Celia looked up to his face to find him grinning at her—a devilish, knowing grin. "Wanna help?" he asked.

"You think entirely too much of yourself, Mr. Putman."

He cocked his head and a finger of his dark hair fell on the long, taut muscles of his shoulder. He licked his bottom lip where the cut was, and his grin broadened. Standing there shirtless, in jeans that clung to his lean hips and long thighs and everything else with indecent exactitude, he was the very personification of the kind of exterior the devil would use to tempt a woman into selling her soul. "No," he said, lifting his T-shirt and pushing his head through. "Just that I know my area of expertise pretty well."

Celia rolled her eyes, refusing to give him the satisfaction of asking what his area of expertise might be. She had a feeling it wasn't the harmonica.

He laughed. "If you like the heat, sugar, I sure hate to see what the cold does to your temper."

She lifted her hair off her neck. "I just want to get out there and plant my garden, start my summer."

"Mmm." He nodded. "All the same, you might want to find something else to put on. Those jeans have to be killing you."

For a minute, she wished she had something wicked, something so skimpy he'd be sorry he'd recommended she put on something cooler. Then she frowned. Why the sudden combativeness?

She closed her eyes briefly, as if she could erase her desire and start afresh. But it even annoyed her that he was right: the jeans *were* uncomfortable, as was the long-sleeved shirt. Her waist was sweaty, her back beneath the elastic of her bra crawled and her calves itched. In the hurry to bring supplies to the attic, she had completely overlooked the need for fresh clothing.

Eric had been digging in the trunk with her grandmother's old clothes and he tossed a simple, sleeveless shift at her. "Go on and change," he urged. Then more kindly he added, "We're bound to be stuck here at least until morning. You may as well get comfortable."

With a sigh, Celia nodded. It wasn't his fault he bewildered her. He hadn't asked to be marooned in an attic with a skinny, boring math teacher. It wasn't his fault that she was so vividly attracted to him. He probably thought he was being kind by keeping her at arm's length.

She grasped the dress and headed for the landing.

By sunset, the attic was stuffy, hot and still. Eric had found a pair of cut-off jean shorts—badly wrinkled and worn nearly threadbare—in his pack. He had exchanged them for his jeans and he was still uncomfortable.

Celia sat by the window, eating stale bread. Her pale skin was flushed and dewy. Her hair, bedraggled by the days without a wash and the effects of the thick air, clung to her neck. The shift she wore was a couple of sizes too big. It gaped around the arms and slipped around the shoulders. She had to keep tugging it up.

She looked like a ragamuffin child in her bare feet and big dress and uncombed hair. It touched him inexplicably, and although he'd kept his distance all day with a combination of humor and silence, he reached now for the comb and a length of string in his pack. "Come here, Celia."

Her big, gray eyes met his and he saw again the strange combination of distrust and hero worship that he'd seen this morning. Ignoring it, he held up his comb. "Let me get your hair out of your way for you."

She seemed to consider this, then stood up and sat down in front of him, tucking the big dress between her knees modestly. He chuckled.

"What?" she asked suspiciously.

He began to untangle her fine hair, gently loosening snarls from the bottom up. "Wonder how old that dress is."

"At least twenty years. I remember it from when I was little." She shrugged. "I know it looks silly, but I don't care. It feels much better than those jeans."

He grunted in answer. The tangles smoothed, he simply combed through the fine mass, admiring the shape of her head and the shine of moon colors through the teeth of his black comb.

For the first time all day, she relaxed. He could see it in the way her shoulders dropped slightly, letting the dress slide out of place once again, showing a spaghetti-thin bra strap. When she reached to pull the fabric again, he said, "Don't worry about that. I've already seen it thirteen times. Just relax."

Surprisingly, she let her hands drop back to her lap. "That really feels good," she admitted. "No one has combed my hair since this dress was new, probably."

The small confession plucked at him. "I used to do my sister's hair before we went to school," he said. "She liked to wear it in one long braid, and it took me a month of Sundays, but I finally got it right."

He divided the silvery hair, remembering Laura's long, thick, black tresses as he began to braid. The back of Celia's arms rested lightly against his bare knees and shins. "Bear with me, now," he said. "It may take me a try or two. It's been a while."

And because his fingers were no longer deft and nimble, the hair fell from his grip more than once. Celia didn't move, and on the fourth try, he managed to weave a smooth braid that he tied with string.

She touched the bow at the end and glanced over her shoulder at him, smiling. "Thanks."

"You're welcome."

With a sigh, less restless now, she reached for the fat candle and lit it, then stood up and helped herself to the bottle of bourbon. "Do you mind?" she asked.

"Not if you'll pour me one while you're at it."

"Of course." She poured, then handed him one cup and curled her hands around the other. Settling opposite him with her back against the wall, she commented, "It's a good thing this is almost over or we'd starve."

He sipped gratefully of the sweet whiskey and settled back himself, leaning his elbows against the mattress. "Yeah, I'm lookin' forward to a big, fat, juicy sirloin, medium rare."

"Mmm." Celia pursed her lips. "I want a meat loaf with ketchup, a pile of buttered string beans and about three pots of very strong coffee."

"Meat loaf?"

"With onions and oatmeal."

He grinned, feeling the whiskey ease down his throat and pool in a dangerous lake of heat in his stomach, a heat he felt move in his blood as her dress slipped again. "Nobody loves meat loaf, Celia. Meat loaf is what your mom made and when you came in for supper you said, 'Oh, no, not meat loaf.'"

She laughed, showing the brilliant, pretty teeth. "My mother wouldn't have come within three feet of a meat loaf. It was what my father and I ate when we were being rebellious."

"And I thought my childhood was strange," Eric said. In spite of the danger, he drank again, feeling a little reckless. A sliver of her very ordinary, very plain white bra showed, and he wondered if she wore ordinary white underwear, as well. Probably. Why the hell should that be so exciting?

"Did you have a strange childhood, Eric?"

"Not like yours. No paparazzi following me around or anything."

"So what made it strange?"

He saw that both of their cups were empty and he lifted the Jack Daniel's bottle to refill them. It was their last night in the attic, after all. They'd been through a flood together. What was a little intemperance between friends? His pouring was generous. "It wasn't exactly strange," he said. "Just bad."

To offset the gloomy sound of that, he picked up his harmonica, but when he blew a few notes, they came out sounding just like his childhood: motherless and full of too much work. He put it down again.

"How long have you played?" Celia asked.

"Harmonica?" he asked before he remembered she didn't know he'd ever played guitar. "Since I was about twelve or so. An old man gave it to me."

"Will you play something?"

He held the harp between his fingers for a moment, hesitating. Then he propped his elbows on his knees and bowed into the instrument, drawing softly. He let the notes lead him where they would. It was again a lonely sound that filled the air, a sound of train whistles in the middle of the night, a sound of empty all-night diners and hotel rooms just before dawn.

His lips tightened and he put the harp down, feeling the old hollowness suck all the breath from his lungs. Celia was silent, but he felt her sympathy as clearly as if she'd wrapped herself around him. He didn't dare look at her. Instead, he ran his thumbs over the engraved silver of the harmonica until the emptiness eased.

How did she know? he wondered. How could she see inside of him the way she did? He didn't like it, didn't like anyone coming that close.

He frowned and looked up. Instead of the flow of kindness he'd seen this morning, there was now a glimmer of amusement in her eyes. One corner of her pretty pink mouth curled almost impishly. Without a word, she grabbed the bottle of bourbon and unstoppered it, then poured a hefty measure in the empty cup near his foot.

Then she returned to her original spot, lifted her cup ironically and took a sip. "I can't help it, you know."

"Help what?" His tone was gruff even to his own ears.

"Seeing what you play. Seeing that you aren't that gruff bad boy you're trying so hard to convince me that you are." The small curl on her mouth broke into a full smile. "I've been teaching for five years. There's always one like you."

The easy observation annoyed him. Deliberately, he eyed the smooth, long expanse of white thigh exposed by her new position. And for an instant, he remembered the feel of her body against his this morning, the easy pearling of her nipple against his hand, the small movements she made against her will. Instinctively, he knew she would be unlike any lover he had ever had.

Lifting the whiskey, he drank it all in one quick swallow, then stood up. "I'm no teenager, Miss Moon."

The glitter of mischievousness in her pale eyes sharpened. She eyed his bared legs and chest, then looked him square in the eye. "I can see that."

He knew if he wanted it, they could be lovers to-night. She didn't exactly expect it, but she'd meet him more than halfway if he let down his walls.

He didn't dare. Not because she'd ask more than he had to give her, not because he didn't want to use this gentle, trusting woman, and not because he could see that she thought herself to be a little infatuated with him.

He could not take that step toward her and lose himself in the delight of exploring her because Celia Moon saw through him—and if he didn't get away real soon, she would see exactly what there was inside of him.

Nothing.

So in spite of the delicious length of thigh and the glitter in her wide, gray eyes and the temptation of her mischievousness, he turned away. "I'm beat," he said, and flopped belly first on the bed, hiding his arousal and his face.

Shutting her out.

Chapter Five

When Celia awakened in the morning, it took her a few seconds to realize what was wrong. Then the complete silence of the room penetrated her fuzzy morning brain.

Eric was gone.

She sat up, her heart squeezing painfully. She'd been so sure he'd at least tell her goodbye.

After a moment of piercing—and disturbing—sorrow over his departure, she spied his pack near the window. His clothes had been gathered, his cards and dice and various other possessions neatly resettled in the heavy canvas pack. Her sadness lightened a notch, but only a notch. The idyll was over. Her drifter was moving on.

She rose and went to the window. Beneath a sunny morning sky, the ground was muddy and strewed with debris of all kinds, put patently, perfectly visible again. A flock of crows picked gleefully through the mud, cawing and chatting and fluttering over the rich finds.

Her sense of depression broke, and she whirled, stopping only to pull on her shoes in clumsy haste. She flew down the stairs and headed for the open front door, anxious to be once again outside, breathing fresh air, feeling the sun on her arms, the wind on her face.

But in the living room, she halted, stunned, her feet sunk in mud.

"Good heavens," she breathed.

She had known, intellectually at least, that water had covered every inch of the house downstairs. She had known things would be ruined, that essentially, she would have to replace everything.

She had not even begun to imagine the complete, utter *mess*.

Mud, twigs, rocks and unidentifiable sludge clung to everything—the furniture and tables, the walls and windowsills and doors. On the floor, the returning water had left swirling footprints of thick silt.

And the smell! She covered her mouth and nose with her hand. It smelled like river water and sodden wood and old carpets; like sewage and stagnant wells.

From just outside the window, a bullfrog croaked, loudly. It startled her and she moved toward the sound.

"Celia! Don't move!" Eric's voice sounded behind her, it's husky tones sharp with warning. "Stay where you are."

Celia froze at the implicit danger in his words. Her mind raced. River water, silt, bullfrogs, snakes. Snakes. Her flesh squeezed on her bones and she shuddered inwardly.

"Don't move one tiny muscle," Eric warned quietly. A soft weight crossed one of her feet, then touched the other. The weight slid with warm, sinuous ease over her shoes. It seemed to go on and on and on. Tears sprung to her eyes as she clenched her fists tight at her sides and gritted her teeth until she thought they would break.

"Keep still, sugar," Eric said, his voice slower now, more seductive than she'd ever heard it. "One more minute."

There was a sudden loud thud and Eric made a peculiar grunting noise. "All right, Celia. You're safe."

It took a minute to unfreeze all the rigid muscles, but Celia creakily turned. At the sight of the creature that had crawled over her feet, now quite obviously dead, she nearly fainted.

"What is that?" she squeaked.

"Haven't you ever seen a water moccasin?" he asked, nudging the body with the shovel he'd used to kill it.

She stared at the mud-colored body, horrified. It was nearly five feet long. No wonder it had taken so long to cross her feet.

She whirled and ran outside, her skin crawling, her stomach heaving. The bullfrog croaked again, and in blind terror, Celia climbed onto the porch railing, clinging to the slippery post rather than take a chance on another snake showing up.

Shivering, she crouched there. She heard Eric come outside, then felt his presence behind her. "You're all right now," he said.

"That's what you think," she said, but her voice was steady. Slowly, her quaking nerves returned to normal and she became aware of the absurd picture she made clinging to the porch railing like a little girl in an oversize dress with unbrushed hair. She looked around the porch, saw that it was empty and gingerly stepped down, trying to reclaim her dignity. "Thank you," she said, head bent.

"I hated to kill him."

Celia choked. "Why?"

"He just got lost. Wasn't his fault old Jezebel threw a temper tantrum and left him stranded in somebody's house." Hands on his hips, Eric looked at the body of the snake, which he'd tossed out into the yard. "Problem is, he doesn't speak English and I don't speak snake."

Celia finally became aware that he'd obviously been working for quite some time this morning. His shirt hung open, his jeans were grimy and a sheen of sweat covered his chest and face. Even so, he was the most incredibly perfect human being she'd ever seen.

He gestured toward the house. "Come on in here and let me show you a couple of things."

"Do you think there will be more snakes?"

"I doubt it, but I'll look around for you before I go."

She nodded.

"Meanwhile, I want you to know what's going on, so come here."

Celia followed him inside, trying to ignore the mud and mess. The sheer work involved in making the house look normal again was daunting

"I used a garden hose to wash out the bathroom so you can use it. The toilet may not be real reliable for a week or two because the lines get clogged—but they'll clear." He wiped a hand over his eyes and gestured toward the far-from-sparkling, but usable room. "At least you can take showers, but it'll drain real slow, too, so make 'em short."

Celia sighed. A shower. "Thank you, Eric."

He moved again, businesslike and to the point. "Come on, there's more." He led her down a hall to the backyard. "The porch steps got washed away," he warned, "so just jump down this way."

Celia followed. He pointed to a section of the foundation under the kitchen. "I checked everything all the way around, and this here's the only problem. Water washed away a lot of the mortar in these stones and you're gonna have to get somebody out here to fix it right, but in the meantime, I braced it with these two-by-fours."

Impressed that he'd even thought to look for foundation damage or to hose down the bathroom or that he knew that the drains would run slowly for a while, Celia nodded. "I really appreciate it."

He shrugged and headed around the house. "Judging by what we got, it'll be a while before anybody can make these little repairs for you, and I wanted to make sure you'd be okay." His tone was gruff. He pointed to a window in the kitchen that had a flat piece of plywood nailed neatly over it. "I got that one open before she flooded, but I guess a rock or something got it anyway."

"I can't believe I slept through you nailing and sawing."

"You were out like light this morning." He raised a devilish eyebrow. "Old Jack'll do that."

She flushed slightly, then raised her own eyebrows. "You should know."

"That I do." Eric bent his head and his wavy black hair fell over his forehead. He shifted from foot to foot for a moment, but Celia just waited.

"You aren't gonna be able to use the lower level for a while, not until they get somebody in with a fire hose to clean it out. You're gonna need a fan or something in that attic or you'll suffocate."

"Okay." Not that she knew if there would even be one available. "I can use my garden hose on the kitchen, right?"

He nodded. "I turned the breakers off at the back of the house, just to let everything dry out. There probably won't be any power for at least a few days, but it's a good idea to leave everything off anyway."

"All right." She smiled. "I wish I could offer you breakfast for your trouble."

"I'll take a rain check," he said in his gravelly voice. "Meantime, I better get on the road and find out how my sister is."

He wouldn't take a rain check, Celia knew. Once he walked away from here, she would never see him again. What was that old song about rolling stones?

Whatever. As Eric went back inside to fetch his backpack, she knew it applied. He was a rolling stone, a drifter with restless feet, and he'd no more hang his hat in one spot than her father had. Seemed to be a prevalent trait in the men from Gideon.

Celia looked at the pecan trees, giant and fruitful. She crossed her arms. Let them wander, then. Here, in this peaceful farmhouse, she'd finally found security and a certain contentment. When the ground dried a little, she would go ahead with her plans for her garden. She'd clean and repair her grandmother's house, repaint and renew and do whatever it took. Let them wander. Celia had found her home.

When Eric returned, she was collecting twigs, branches and assorted trash and putting it all into a pile. She held up a pair of pants, practically new. "She'll eat anything, won't she?"

Eric gave Celia a reluctant grin. "You better believe it." He came down the stairs, loose limbed and sexy as a movie star, even with the grime of the days just past and his morning's work clinging to him. In the sunshine, his dark blue eyes glowed nearly sapphire, and whatever her resolve, Celia couldn't help the leap of her belly at the sight.

His pack was firmly hiked over his shoulder. "I looked from one end of the house to the other and didn't find any more snakes. Put a rope on the steps if it'll make you feel better."

"A rope?"

He lifted one shoulder. "Supposedly they won't cross a rope."

"It's worth a try," she said.

"Well." He glanced down the road, shifted his weight, looked at Celia. "Guess I'll be heading out now."

Celia tossed the pants she'd found onto the porch, thinking they'd wash up and be good for something. She looked at him. Nodded.

"Want to thank you for taking me in," he said.

Her heart sped up a little. "My pleasure." A sense of sorrow and lost chances washed over her. She looked at his face very carefully, trying to imprint it forever upon her memory—his full lips and black hair, the harsh planes and rough dark beard shadowing a hard jaw. Her chest ached when she looked into his jeweled and lonely eyes.

It was again a scene torn from one of her father's books. She was playing the wistful heroine right down to the ache in her heart.

Jacob Moon's scenarios be damned. Without knowing she would, she walked up to Eric and put her hand on his cheek. "You are the most beautiful man I have ever seen, Eric Putman," she said in a soft voice.

Then because she couldn't stand to let him walk away without kissing him just once, she stood on her toes and when that wasn't enough, tugged his big head down gently to hers.

Their lips met and Celia felt his surprise in the sudden softness in his mouth, in the off-center way he met her. There was no resistance in him, only that broad and oddly vulnerable surprise.

And if her heart had ached before, it now pounded with a virulent and shattering pain. His hair was thick against her fingers, his body broad and strong, his mouth tender and firm as a nectarine.

After a moment, he let the pack slide from his shoulder and with a small, low growl, he pulled her into him, shifting his head to suckle gently at her lips. This time, his arms were not loose around her. His hands splayed possessively over her back, and his arms curled with power around her shoulders, pulling her so close that her breasts were nearly crushed against his ribs.

And his mouth—his mouth. Celia tilted her head against the crook of his elbow, feeling the hard press of his biceps against her ear as his mouth tenderly explored hers. His tongue teased for entrance and Celia parted her lips to give it, feeling reason spin away as they tangled and danced together. His chest was pressed so closely to hers that she could feel his heartbeat, deep and thrumming, and a small but discernible tremble quivering through his limbs.

For a moment he ceased, pulling back an inch or two, and his broad, scarred hand cupped her cheek. His sapphire eyes glittered with something lost and sad and so hungry that Celia felt her own body shaking with the need to fill it. For a long moment she felt suspended in that painful, jeweled gaze, and then he lowered his head once more to kiss her mouth with such gentleness, it bordered on reverence. He kissed her slowly, then touched her nose and both cheeks, letting her go an inch at time, until somehow they were standing separate again, facing each other in the bright light of a Texas morning. "Goodbye, Celia," he said, his voice rasping almost below register.

She swallowed. "Bye," she whispered.

He hitched his pack onto one shoulder and strode off down the muddy road without a backward glance. Celia watched him, her heart pounding. She was glad she had kissed him, that she would carry always the memory of it.

Because she would never see him again. And considering everything, that was probably a very good thing. A man like that . . .

Setting her jaw, she turned back to the work that awaited her. Her life had been filled with dangerous turns and instability. A man like that would only bring more of the same.

Eric found Laura's house deserted.

The front door was unlocked, as if she'd been waiting for him. The living room carpet was freshly vacuumed, the pillows on the couch plumped and artfully arranged. In the spare bedroom, the coverlet had been turned back to show crisp, fresh linens, and in the ice box were hot dogs and cheese and a jug of sweet tea.

He paced around the rooms for a little while, noting these details, wondering if she'd just stepped out for a minute now that the water had receded. But why hadn't she left him a note, then?

He showered off the grime of the past few days from his body, and drank some of the tea. He was starving—the flood provisions had not been the best to start with and after three days of peanut butter and crackers, his stomach ached for something real. There was no electricity here, either, so he had to content himself with several bowls of cold cereal. They helped.

It was only as his stomach stopped growling that he realized Laura had not been in the house since the flood started. There were candles on the kitchen and bedside tables, each with a book of matches alongside. Several cans of Sterno were piled next to a fondue pot on the counter, and an ice chest beside the refrigerator awaited a power failure.

But the food had not been spoiled. The tea was lukewarm, but he'd found a handful of useable ice cubes left in their trays. Because the doors had not been opened since the power failed, they held in the cold for much, much longer.

The candles hadn't been lit. Not even once.

A sickening sense of panic built in his belly. He fought it with reason. Laura had chosen this house because it sat on the west side of Jezebel, on a bluff. The river nearly always jumped her banks to the east, and the bluff was fifteen feet, providing protection even if the river climbed her west bank.

Eric peered out the kitchen window. His sister had known the river was on the rise. She had also known Eric was on his way. He had called her the morning of his arrival, that gloomy rainy morning. She had prepared for both the flood and his arrival.

And then she'd left the house?

It made no sense whatsoever. Feeling sick, he headed for the door.

He spent the day trying to find traces of where she might have gone. The going was rough. Hardly anyone, thanks to the flood, was where they might have been ordinarily. The phone lines were down. Electricity had yet to be restored, and the roads were covered with silt, branches and an occasional hapless animal.

It soon became obvious he would not even be able to find out who had last seen her until things had been restored to some kind of order, and to keep himself from worrying, he hiked down the road to see what might have become of his car. He took back roads and shortcuts he'd known since childhood in order to avoid the sight of Celia's farmhouse.

To his great surprise, he found the car relatively untouched, jammed hard against a tree only a few feet from where he'd left it. The windows weren't even broken, although enough water had seeped in through little crevices to give the whole interior a smell of river silt.

A dent from a tree branch or rock marred the driver's door, but other than that, the body looked sound. He lifted the hood and stared at the engine.

Staring was about all he could do. Like mathematics, engine functions had always been just beyond his ken. He could change a spark plug if the need arose, fill the various reservoirs and identify problems by the sounds they made, but that was as far as it went.

At least the car hadn't been washed down river. He was attached to the Volvo. It was the best car he'd ever owned and had served him well for two years, since his old car...

He shut off that line of thought with clenched teeth.

One thing he did know was that the distributor cap had to be dry. He tugged it off and dried it, then tried to turn the engine over. Nothing. Which meant the carburetor might have gotten wet. He'd have to leave it until someone from a garage could tow the car in and check it out.

The last thing he did was open the back door to get the guitar he'd left on the seat. Throughout the flood, he'd cursed his choice to leave it behind, in spite of the fact that it was essentially useless to him. Wild Willie Hormel had given him the '57 Stratocaster when Eric was fifteen, and even if he never played it again, he wanted to keep it. He didn't understand exactly what had made him leave it in the first place, except a certain panic—reminders of rainy nights he had done his best to forget.

The black case was gone. He stared at the vacant place in the seat with a sense of terrible loss for an instant.

Then he straightened, his jaw hard. No more illusions. The guitar, like Retta and his old car, was gone, along with everything else that had existed before that night.

Except Laura.

Stonily, he closed the door and the hood and headed back toward his sister's place.

As night crept in, he found himself drawn outside to the porch. The long day was catching up with him and he settled on a kitchen chair in the hot night, putting his feet up on the rail. In the dahlia bushes nestled around the small bungalow, crickets whirred and chirped, and the sounds of Jezebel came faintly, rushing through the night. Above the silhouettes of pine trees across the road rose the moon, round and pale, nearly full.

Silver light shone over the road, the color of a woman's hair, the color of her big eyes. Fey Celia.

Eric plucked the harmonica from his shirt pocket. A shroud of clouds crossed the moon, giving it an ominous aspect, and Eric felt a ripple of foreboding shoot through his chest.

Where was Laura?

He knew with the certainty that stemmed from his own terrifying memories of the last flood that she would not have ventured out with the river on the rise. He'd been six, Laura nine, when Jezebel had swept them into her skirts. What he remembered in bits and pieces, Laura remembered in acute detail.

She wouldn't have gone out. Not voluntarily.

Restlessly, he walked out to the road and stared down the long, dark ribbon of blacktop as if he could make her materialize. He swore and paced back to the porch, knowing he'd be unable to sleep.

Every time he came back to Gideon, something happened. Bad things, most often. The last time, just after the accident, he'd come home to find Laura married, her husband so jealous, he didn't even want Eric talking to her. Last time, in the hardware store, Retta's cousin had called him a murderer.

He paced, thinking it had only been last night he had sat with Celia in her attic, braiding her hair. It had been only this morning she had stood on her tiptoes to kiss him goodbye.

Her kiss. Sweet as honeysuckle, rich as cream. He'd hardly known how to respond to a kiss given so freely, without demands or conditions attached. No expectations or wiles or hidden motives had marred that offering. So simple, as simple as her words, which echoed in memory no matter how he tried to push them away. *You're the most beautiful man I've ever seen.*

Her generosity had slipped through his guard as nothing else could have. For the space of long moments, Eric had been free to take what she offered. He remembered the brush of her hair on his arms, the press of her breasts and hips, the rainbow taste of her plump mouth.

As he remembered, he drew on his harmonica without much direction. The notes leapt out into the night and hearing them, Eric grinned to himself. In his mind's eye, he saw a picture of Cinderella in the Disney movie, surrounded by tiny bluebirds and all kinds of other little creatures.

He chuckled, amazed that so much of the romantic in him had managed to survive.

Then he sobered, remembering the end of that kiss, the trembling that had shook him, the devouring hunger he'd felt. A hunger that had gone far, far beyond a need for sexual release. As she had nestled against him, Eric had wished with all his being that he had something to offer her, something to give. His body had trembled with the wish to be someone else, anyone else, someone who was right for that sweet and gentle woman. Someone worthy of her.

Because Eric Putman was not. He had nothing. Once, he might have offered her pleasure, but Retta had taught him how destructive that could be. No amount of passion ever made up for love.

Whatever happened the next few days, he had to keep reminding himself of that.

Chapter Six

The high school, a structure built of native stone at the turn of the century, served as the Red Cross station. The gymnasium was turned into an emergency shelter for those left homeless, and the auditorium was lined with long tables and folding chairs where Red Cross volunteers handed out food, clothing, supplies and information.

After four days of volunteer work, Celia felt like an old hand. In spite of the mess still littering her farmhouse, she felt grateful as she handed out clothes from the Salvation Army to entire families who had lost everything in the flood. She counted her blessings as she served stews to mothers with children clinging to their skirts. At night when she returned to the intimidating reality of just exactly how long it would take to get things together in the house, she was grateful that Eric had appeared at the right moment to urge her to move the mattress from her bed upstairs.

She was also grateful for the bone-deep weariness that let her sleep without dreams.

Now, at the end of the fourth day, she sorted a box of clothes by size and sex, rubbing absently at an ache in her lower back.

A tall black woman, dressed in the apron she'd donned over her clothes to help prepare the evening meal, plopped down in the chair beside Celia. "Hey, lady."

Celia looked up and smiled. Lynn taught geography and history and had a reputation for being the toughest teacher in Texas. Except for Celia. Their reputations had given them an instant bond. "You've got flour on your nose," she said.

Lynn brushed at it distractedly, her wooden bracelets clacking on her arm. "You about to finish up there?"

"I hope so. I don't think I have a single brain cell still functioning."

"I know what you mean." Lynn untied her apron. "I'm thinking I'd like an escape. Are you game?"

"Hmm," Celia said, folding a baby's sleeper. "Sometimes your schemes leave a little to be desired in the sanity realm."

"Oh, I'm too tired to be reckless. I was thinking about going over to the blues joint tonight. You ever been there?"

Celia felt a ripple of excitement, thinking of the pictures Eric's harmonica had called up in her mind. "No, I never have."

Lynn raised an eyebrow. "Your daddy used to hang out there, I'm told."

"I'd love it. Let's go."

"I'll pick you up about ten." Lynn stood up, tucking a lock of hair into place.

"Ten?"

"If we wanted to be hip, we wouldn't show until midnight, but I'm afraid I'd fall asleep."

"What should I wear?"

Lynn turned, smiling wickedly. "Well, you don't want to go as a schoolteacher. Think sin."

Celia laughed. "I'll do my best."

What Celia had failed to take into consideration, however, was that most of her clothes, aside from the few everyday pieces she had managed to wash out in the bathtub, were still covered with flood droppings.

She'd bought a pair of stockings at the drugstore on the way home, had showered and done her hair, then gone upstairs to the trunk, smiling to herself.

The dress had belonged to someone other than her grandmother, or else she'd worn it when she was quite, quite young, because it fit Celia exactly. Made of black crepe with a draped neckline, its lines were exquisitely simple, but if ever she'd seen a dress that shouted sin, this was it.

And when Lynn appeared, Celia wasn't disappointed. Electricity had not yet been restored to the outlying farm, and she greeted her friend by the light of a candle. Lynn whistled in admiration. "Honey, I had no idea you could look like that."

"Lacking your voluptuousness, I had to get creative," Celia replied. Lynn's dress, too, was black. Strapless, the silky fabric clung to a dizzying array of curves and stopped midthigh, showing off what Celia's father would have called "racehorse legs." "You ought to be ashamed of yourself, Lynn. Some man is going to have a heart attack and it'll be all your fault."

Batting her eyelashes, Lynn struck a pose. "I know," she said sweetly.

Celia laughed.

The club was nestled on a small bluff on the western bank of the river. A simple wooden structure settled obscurely in the middle of a clearing, it hardly looked like anything to Celia. No sign marked the exterior. "It sure doesn't look like any nightclub I've ever seen."

"It's not," Lynn promised.

It wasn't. But the instant Celia stepped through the door, she knew she'd at last found her father's Gideon. Small, simple tables cluttered the open room, many of them filled despite what Lynn implied was a very early hour. The only lights in the room were over the long, long wooden bar against one wall and over a small stage that was empty at the moment, although a collection of instruments and microphones stood waiting.

Someone had put quarters in the jukebox, and a Billie Holiday song floated through the air, hazy and dark, adding to the mood of the smoky, hot room.

Celia turned and squeezed her companion's arm. "Oh, Lynn," she whispered, "this is great!"

Lynn's attention had caught on something and a soft, ripe smile touched her mouth. "I'm inclined to agree."

Celia followed her gaze. Not something—someone; an impossibly tall man with the shoulders of a fullback and a clean-shaven chin was bent over a table, talking with two other men. All three were as shiny clean as new pennies, and Celia knew they'd smell like heaven. "Who is he?" she asked as Lynn led the way to a small open table near the dance floor.

"David West. He's just come back from Dallas to work for the Sheriff's Department."

"Nice-looking," Celia commented.

"No." Lynn shook her head. "Nice-looking is a car. Nice-looking is your grandpa." Her eyes fastened on David. "That's drop-dead gorgeous."

Drop-dead gorgeous. Celia bent her head, her vision suddenly filled with a memory of Eric standing in her attic without his shirt, casually touching his chest.

She had told no one that he'd been there. Not even Lynn, although a part of her now wanted to. She wanted to say, "Speaking of gorgeous, did I tell you about the man marooned with me for two days and nights during the flood? Did I happen to mention I can't stop thinking about him even though I know I'll never see him again?"

But she didn't. She ordered a drink—Jack Daniel's, neat—and watched the waitress turn her lips down in surprise. It gave Celia almost the same satisfaction she got by telling people she taught calculus.

The band eased out of the crowd and assembled on the stage by ten, laughing and joking among themselves with the easy camaraderie of long acquaintance. The leader was old, with long lines in his dark face and grizzlings of white in his hair. He slipped a guitar strap over his head and glanced at the other members of the group—a trumpet player as skinny as a cattail, a bass player arched like a bow and a piano player even older than the guitarist. They ambled into their music, starting off slow and easy. The club settled in anticipation, and Celia felt a strange, electric clutch catch her chest. She sipped gingerly at the whiskey in her glass.

The guitarist led, both with his instrument and his rough voice. Woven through his lead was the mournful saxophone, whining like a cold wind one minute, chuckling like a fat man the next.

The songs were about lost love and mean women and hard times—and yet, Celia, falling adrift in the seduction of the sounds, felt the celebration in them, too. Lynn got up to dance, leaving Celia alone at the table to analyze the surprising notion of the blues being a celebration. Everything she'd ever believed about them said otherwise.

But it was hard to maintain an analytical mood amid the seductive sounds that filled the room. Even for Celia. Her instinctive need to take things apart slipped away under the force of the pictures dancing all over the room, pictures like those Eric had given her with his harmonica. No two were alike, and as Celia glanced around at the other patrons tapping their feet and smiling and moving their heads in time with the music, she knew her pictures were not quite the same as anyone else's.

She smiled and lifted her glass, only to find it empty. Surprised, she glanced over her shoulder for the waitress to order another.

And froze. For there, perched on a stool, his elbows bent against the bar, was Eric. At the now-familiar shock his face always gave her, a sense of relief washed through her. He was still here. And she'd known somehow that she might find him in the steamy blues club. He'd flashed through her mind the instant Lynn had suggested it.

In just a few days, Celia had forgotten again how startlingly beautiful he was. Pale yellow light from behind the bar spilled over his hair, neatly combed away from his clean-shaven face, and he wore a Civil War style shirt with his time-whitened jeans.

An ache struck her belly and quivered through her nerves. Every time she looked at him, she wanted to make love. She wanted to feel his big body wrapped around hers, wanted to lose herself in his lonely, sapphire eyes. She wanted to crack the walls he kept between himself and the world, and instinctively she knew the only way it would happen was in bed.

Hearing her thoughts, she was mildly shocked. But somehow, under the spell of the music and the thick heat that filled the room, it seemed as natural to think of making love as to drink water to quench her thirst.

As she watched, his jaw went hard and he lifted his glass with a stony expression, his gaze unwaveringly fixed upon the band. Celia wondered suddenly what his story was, what he had lost to put such a yearning in his eyes. She wanted to learn the details of his life, then set about soothing the pain from each and every one.

But unlike her dreamy vision of making love, this wish gave her a jolt—had she lost her mind? She'd spent too much time with stormy, moody people to miss identifying one now. Whatever he'd lost, it had to do with the blues.

Squaring her shoulders, she turned back toward the band. The last thing in the world she wanted was to get mixed up with somebody who could get that kind of an expression on his face.

Eric swallowed more whiskey, hoping to ease the panic in his chest. Four days he'd been looking for his sister, and in four days he'd found no trace of her.

Today, braving the shops in town, he had learned a fact more chilling than her disappearance. Her ex-husband was missing, too—the very same jealous husband who'd thrown fits about Eric the last time he'd been in town. Jake Gaines was a mean son of gun, a fact Laura had learned too late.

Eric cursed inwardly. The reason he'd come to Gideon this time had been to stay with Laura for a while, until Jake got the message that Laura was finished with him.

"Doin' all right there, son?" the bartender asked, wiping the bar down alongside Eric's half-full glass.

Eric nodded. "Fine, thanks."

The bartender, not to be dissuaded, leaned on the wide, polished wood surface. "Come on now," he said, gesturing toward the musicians. "Man's supposed to leave his troubles at the door when he comes in the Five O'Nine.'' He winked. ''Ain't nothing a pretty woman can't make you forget—for a little while, anyway.''

Eric grinned reluctantly. ''Some troubles, my friend, grab on to your ankle and follow you in.''

The bartender pursed his lips and nodded. ''Like that, is it?''

Then, hailed by a waitress, the gold-toothed man headed away. Eric watched him go, thinking maybe he was right. A woman, a little dancing, a little whiskey...

But even as he scanned the crowd, he knew it was futile. The only way to ease this trouble was to find his sister.

A flash of moon-colored hair, bright in the dimness of the club, caught his eye. And despite himself, Eric felt a leap of anticipation, a sudden lightness amid the thickness of worry in his chest. He shifted, and the couple blocking his view obligingly got up to dance, leaving him a clear view.

It was Celia, all right. Eric felt a pang, seeing her, and he remembered the calm of her attic, the quiet peace they had shared even amid the storm. It was an absurdly nostalgic emotion and, annoyed, Eric shoved it away.

This Celia was nothing like the girl in the oversize shift he'd left at the farmhouse. This Celia wore a black dress that showed her collarbone and a lot more chest than he would have thought she'd allow. The fabric clung to her modest curves and small waist like a lover, and when she stood up to allow a group to pass by in the slender aisle, he saw that it did amazing things for the fine, round little fanny.

He shifted and without taking his eyes from her, lifted his glass to swallow a brace of Jack Daniel's. Her legs, too, were pretty, elegant in the silky casing of black stockings.

Admiring her fine shape and graceful movement, Eric remembered the mischievousness in her eyes, remembered her kiss, remembered how her breast had exactly fit his palm, as if the two were made to meet. An abrupt, insistent heat stirred below his belt.

He wanted her. And if she were willing, what would it hurt? This Celia hardly looked like the innocent he'd believed her to be, and realizing she'd spent her childhood running all over Europe with her parents, he thought maybe that had been a foolish assumption in the first place. She could hardly be as innocent as she appeared.

The bartender returned. "See, now?" he said with a soft chuckle. "She's pretty as sunshine. Don't it feel better?"

Eric smiled and glanced over his shoulder at the man, lifting a rueful eyebrow in agreement. He stood up, about to cross the room to ask her to dance.

But the band ended their song and the musicians took a break, melting into the crowd. Eric shrugged at the bartender.

The man laughed. "Next time," he said.

As Eric settled back on his stool, oddly disappointed, a deep, rough and familiar voice at his side said, "Thought that was you, boy. You gone and got so uppity you can't even say hello?"

Eric turned, grinning. "Wild Willie," he said in greeting, holding out a hand. "How you doin', old man?"

The guitarist who led the band settled on the stool next to Eric, inclining his head. "Can't complain." He smiled, showing a mouthful of extraordinary teeth—teeth he'd been heard to boast of more than once. "You picked a hell of a time to drop by the old hometown."

"Old Jezebel would have waited until I got here to throw her temper tantrum, the way my luck is going."

Willie's eyes, rheumy with his nearly seventy years, sobered. "I heard about the accident," he said. "Hard luck."

Eric nodded curtly, then realized he owed much more than that to the man who'd given him the guitar in the first place, the man who'd taught him all he could absorb. Wild Willie was old now, but once upon a time, he'd played with the best in clubs big and small all over the South. An accident of his own had brought him into Eric's life, and while he'd mended, Willie had taught a restless, hungry boy how to play blues guitar. And more.

Grimly, Eric held up his hands, displaying the riddled mass of scars. "Can't play a lick," he said.

"I'm real sorry, boy. You were one of the best."

It was no idle compliment, and Eric accepted it in the spirit it was offered. "Thanks."

Willie examined him for a minute, and Eric allowed it, feeling the concern and questions behind the twitch of the old man's lips. "Why don't you come on and sing with us? Do you some good."

"Ah, Willie, you know singing was never my thing. Guitar was what I did, and it's gone."

Wild Willie shook his head, smiling fondly. "Boy, the blues don't let you go," he said. "Sooner you know that, better off you gonna be." He clapped Eric on the shoulder, then rose and left him alone.

Eric looked into the amber liquid of his glass, and through the walls of his crumbing defenses, he saw the accident—the rain and dark road, the shrill fury of the woman next to him. He felt anew the anger beating reckless in his chest, felt the rebellious press of his foot on the accelerator, felt the sick lurch of his stomach as the car left the road, sailing like a missile through the wet dark.

Reacting instinctively to protect his eyes, he'd raised his hands.

And for a few moments, there had been only the sound of shattering glass and twisting metal and screams cutting through the dark as the car smashed into a tree. Eric had been thrown clear through the windshield. Retta had not been so lucky.

The thought still made him sick. Much as he'd hated her in those moments before the crash, he would never have wished her dead.

He flexed his hands, so hungry to play, it was a physical pain. It hadn't been much of a life. As much as he'd loved losing himself in the blues, he hated the constant travel it required, the late nights in strange places, the loneliness, that even with Retta—hell, even more with Retta—followed him like a faithful dog. He'd hated the life.

But, Lord, he missed the blues.

As if in emphasis, Willie's guitar sung out, alone, a bottle-neck slide whining over the strings in an exact rendition of the loneliness in Eric's heart. Eric turned to watch, knowing that sad chord was for him.

But instead of easing his mood, the song only pulled him deeper into his despair. He'd come here tonight looking for something nameless, something he'd found here once upon a time. Instead, all he'd found was that he had lost everything.

Abruptly, he stood up to yank bills from the front pocket of his jeans, needing urgently to escape. The money caught on a seam and he had to struggle to get it out. Just as it came free, a gentle pressure fell on his arm.

"Don't go," Celia said.

Startled he looked at her, taking in the low sweep of her black dress, a black that made her hair and eyes and skin seem even paler by comparison. Anyone else with her coloring would have looked dead in black. Celia looked ethereal, fey, magic—as if she had some inner light.

"Dance with me," she said quietly.

In her big, gray eyes was a shadow of the hero worship he'd seen before, an innocent kind of expression completely at odds with the message of her dress and her unconsciously seductive movements.

He swallowed, a little lost in those eyes. Lord have mercy, he thought vaguely. He wanted to grab her and pull her tight, wanted to escape the fear and hunger and desperation eating away at him like acid. He wanted to bury himself deep in her softness so that he could forget that the last person he had on earth might be dead.

It would be selfish to touch her, knowing it wasn't her he needed. He opened his mouth to refuse, but Celia took his hand. "Just one dance," she coaxed, and then gave him a sweet and somehow very inviting smile. "For old times' sake."

Hell. He melted in the sweetness of her invitation and nodded to her. She took his hand and led him to the dance floor. It was covered in slick linoleum tiles, clean and waxed, but a long way from fancy.

It was hot in the little club, the air steamy with bodies and the heavy rains and the normal east Texas summer heat. A sheen of moisture made Celia's face shine, and he smiled as he took her into his arms loosely. Not too close. "How do you like the sunshine now, sugar?"

"It's hot." She smiled up at him. "Hotter than any jungle, hotter than anything I've ever experienced." She stepped a little closer. "But I still like it."

He smiled in acknowledgment of the afternoon in her attic.

"I like this song," she said.

The truth was, Eric hadn't been listening. It was a smoky, old ballad about a good woman and a bad man—and she was right. It was sultry, especially in Willie's raspy voice. Eric thought about how he'd been known to sing it pretty well himself and half regretted his refusal to sing.

He pulled Celia closer, willing to take the bartender's advice and leave his troubles behind for a minute or two. As the plaintive guitar music circled them, he felt her hands fall onto his waist, felt the moisture and heat that came with such contact in such weather. Their thighs somehow tangled and he could feel the swish of her stockings against the fabric of his jeans. Her flesh was damp, and she smelled of her oddly exotic perfume, patchouli and roses.

He shifted, bowing his face into her hair, feeling it sweep over his mouth and nose. He tugged her closer yet, letting his hands roam over her back and the sway of her waist and to the very edge of her pretty round bottom. He wondered how that flesh would fit his hands.

"Mmm," he growled in her ear. "Celia, you're sweet. You feel so good."

She made no answer, but moved against him, sinuous and innocent and instinctive, and a small, soft sigh escaped her throat.

He smiled. It felt natural to hold her, to contemplate dropping a kiss to her ear or temple, to feel her humming under her breath.

All at once he was flooded with an acute and aching hunger—a hunger for Celia, for the music he'd lost, for a normal life. It welled and filled him from toes to scalp, stinging and sharp and irresistible. It scared him to want anything. To want so much was akin to losing his mind.

And yet he couldn't let her go. He closed his eyes and pressed his mouth into her hair.

The band slid without a break into a new song. Eric paid it little attention at first as the sax and guitar played a mournful intro.

Then Wild Willie's voice growled over the microphone, "This one here's for our local boy."

Eric panicked as Willie began to sing a low and sorrowful ballad of a lonely man, a song Eric knew intimately—every dip and slide and swell. It was famous. It was his favorite.

A cold ache rose in his throat and froze his arms across Celia's back. Abruptly he let go of her. For a minute he stood there, wanting to tell her—

"I'm sorry," he growled, then walked stiffly from the dance floor, unable to face the sound of the life he'd lost.

But even outside in the hot night, the music followed. The wailing sax dove into the splash of Jezebel's skirts against the bank, creating a union that sounded so much like home, it made him want to cry like the boy he'd been when that home had been stolen away. He couldn't breathe. The air was too thick, too hot, too wet.

Why did he ever come home? Every time he came here, he lost control. He'd hated it as a child, when townspeople snubbed his mother so that it was obvious enough for even a six-year-old to understand. He'd hated it when his sister had cried over the names school children called her. He'd hated it when . . .

Always. In Gideon, his walls crumbled and he became as vulnerable as a naked baby bird fallen from its nest. Out there on the road, playing blues or just roaming, at least he had some feathers.

He had to find his sister. And once he found her, he would take her out of Gideon, too, so he never had to come back here again.

As Eric rigidly walked out of the club, Celia stood on the dance floor feeling as oddly deprived as she had the morning he'd rolled away from her, leaving her cold after the heat they'd shared in the middle of her bed.

Remembering the loneliness in his eyes that morning, she frowned. Then forgetting everything else, she followed him out the open door of the Five O'Nine.

In spite of the steaminess of the club, there had been at least a few overhead fans beating the air, moving it around. As she stepped into the night, there was no such luxury. The air struck her like a soft, wet net, clinging to her hair and sticking her dress to her body and making her legs crawl beneath the stockings. For a minute, she couldn't catch her breath and stood just outside the door, looking for Eric.

His figure was shrouded by the shadows of a great, old pine. He was bent over, his hands on his knees, like a man who wanted to rid himself of an evil in his belly. Sorrow rose from him in waves.

She approached quietly and stopped a foot or two away from him. "Who are you?" she asked.

Eric straightened. For a long moment, he stared at her, his jaw hard, his eyes shuttered. "No one you'd want to know, sugar," he said in his rough voice. "Trust me."

Then he turned and strode off into the forest. The darkness swallowed him in an instant. Celia crossed her arms, struck suddenly by two facts.

The night and everything about it was once again reminiscent of one of her father's novels. She and Eric had taken their places and acted them out perfectly— he was the tortured and magnetic drifter; she was the woman drawn irrevocably to his fire, a fire kindled in hell. Even the music now was right, and the air. She felt as though she were trapped in some strange dream from which she couldn't escape.

As disturbing as that was, the second fact was even more so. Even knowing her father would write the scene in just this way, knowing that Eric was obviously a man with a grim past and no future, she couldn't stop thinking about him.

It disgusted her. She'd never liked her father's heroines. They were always passive creatures, at the mercy of storms and men and their own emotions. Victims, every last one of them.

She raised her chin and headed back into the club. She was no victim—and she'd thwart this story line if it was the last thing she did. For a moment, on the threshold of the club, she paused and looked toward the river, toward Jezebel, hearing the seductively calm sound of her waters singing over the rocks in her path.

Jezebel. Celia smiled, feeling a sudden kinship with the river. There might be lessons that a river named Jezebel could teach a woman if she were willing to learn.

She took her seat next to Lynn, strangely fortified.

"How do you know Eric?" Lynn asked.

Celia shook her head, still reluctant to share the story of the flood. "I don't, not really."

Lynn inclined her head. "You look like the cat that swallowed the canary, Celia. Come on. You must have met him before."

"I don't really want to talk about it, okay?"

"Okay." Lynn took a long swallow of her gin and tonic, eyes shining secretively. "Do you know who he is?"

Celia sighed, seeing she would have to listen if she wanted to be finished with the subject. "Should I?"

"I'd say so. He's as much a local hero as your daddy."

Frowning, Celia looked at her.

"That song he walked out on?" Lynn continued. "He wrote it when he was seventeen years old—it's been recorded about a dozen times. And it's just one of many. There are those who say his songs are some of the best of this generation."

Celia uttered an earthy curse. Her heart plummeted. "I would rather he'd been a drifter," she said harshly, then excused herself to go to the ladies' room.

She splashed cold water on her face. It was bad enough that he was physically the most compelling man she'd ever seen, that his eyes were so lonely they made her want to cry, that he was so much like one of her father's heroes she wanted to kill him.

But he was a blues man, a *wandering* blues man. It would be hard to imagine a worse choice.

She tore a paper towel from the dispenser and blotted the moisture from her face, staring at herself in the mirror. Her eyes went hard.

Eric was right. She didn't want to know him.

Chapter Seven

Eric approached the high school with a feeling of dread in the pit of his stomach. A handful of children shimmied up a cottonwood tree Eric remembering climbing himself as a child. He envied them for an instant. If only he were five and Laura eight, playing Robin Hood in the trees.

Inside, there were hand-lettered signs posted on the walls—tempera paint on butcher paper, the same kind of signs he remembered from his short term in these halls. But instead of asking support for glee club or announcing a bake sale, the signs pointed toward various Red Cross stations.

An arrow directed him toward the auditorium, a musty-smelling room with heavy velvet drapes. Eric paused at the doors. A woman passed him, her head down, her face running with tears she couldn't control.

Dread seized him again. *Sweet Jesus,* he prayed. *Don't let her be dead.*

He set his jaw and pushed through the doors. A knot of people on the old wooden stage gathered before a table staffed by several volunteers. One of them was Lynn Williams, a woman he'd known since sixth grade. He joined the line in front of her.

When his turn came, she looked up wearily, and seeing Eric, smiled. "Hello there, stranger. Sit down."

Her friendliness eased the fear in his chest. "Hi, Lynn. How are you doing?"

"Can't complain." She folded her long fingers together. "Is this business or social?"

He took a breath. "Business," he growled, and cleared his throat. "I can't find Laura and—well," he looked at Lynn. "I guess I figured you'd know who was dead."

"Oh, honey." She touched his hand over the table and squeezed his fingers. "Hang on. I'll get the lists."

It seemed to take forever for her to stand up and cross the slats to another small table piled with computer printouts. Eric watched her flip through one stack, then pick up another, her neat, dark head bent over the lists as she walked back. A pulse beat in his ears, thready with terror.

She sat back down and looked at him, shaking her head. "There are three counties affected by the flood. Twelve people are reported dead—four all from one farm down river. Nobody else fits Laura's description." She glanced up. "There's a missing persons list about a page long. I can put her on that, but you may not hear anything for a while.''

Eric nodded. A weakness of relief and renewed worry skimmed his nerves for an instant, making it hard to speak. "Put her on the list.'' He narrowed his eyes. "Is Jake Gaines on there?''

Lynn nodded without even having to check. "His mama and sisters were in here the day the Red Cross got here, screaming about their baby." She rolled her eyes. "Never met such a useless bunch in my life.''

Eric grinned. "Thanks, Lynn.'' He stood up, mindful of the others waiting their turns.

"Don't be such a stranger, now, you hear?" Lynn said, sliding the stacks of paper to one side. "Stop in and have some coffee with me some evenin'.''

He tipped an imaginary hat. "I'll do that.''

As he was about to turn, Celia came through the drapes at the back of the stage, her arms overflowing with rags and sprays and brushes, all kinds of cleaning supplies. Her hair was caught back under a splashy purple bandanna, and her jeans were filthy. He wondered what she'd been doing.

Then her eyes lifted and she caught sight of him, and a sharp, hard spark darkened the silvery irises to a gun-metal gray. Her chin rose.

Eric gave her a quick nod, then pivoted blindly, nearly missed a stair and bolted from the room. There was no other word for it. The damnable thing was, as he stood outside again, he realized that for an instant, he'd really felt a little better.

* * *

Cooking was not an art that had come easily to Celia. Her mother had never entered a kitchen in her life, and her father, being male and Texan, could hustle up pecan pie or biscuits, but nothing substantial. As a result, Celia had spent the past ten years slowly but surely educating herself on the finer points of putting a meal together. It was mathematical and orderly, and she enjoyed the meshing of ingredients that formed a new product. It soothed her.

In the late afternoon after seeing Eric at the school, she baked one of her grandmother's specialties, turtle brownies. It was the first real baking she'd been able to do since the flood, and as the scent of chocolate and caramel and pecans wafted through the newly cleaned kitchen, a sense of ease crept through her. She hummed under her breath as she washed the bowls and spoons, then shook out a paper doily to decorate a plate.

When the brownies had cooled, she cut them into perfect squares and arranged them on the lacy paper, admiring the contrast of dark chocolate against snowy white. Pretty enough for an entry in the fair, she thought, then grinned—as if she'd dare compete with women who'd been cooking for thirty or forty years!

Her grandmother had won first-prize ribbons for watermelon-rind pickles and plum jam and peach chutney every year. Celia remembered sitting on a stool in this very kitchen, listening to injunctions about sterilizing jars and washing the lids with a hot wet cloth; about cutting plums just so and loading slices of fruit into the jars in an even way. She had yet to tackle canning. Maybe this fall.

When the brownies were finished, she showered and changed into a cool cotton sundress, then brushed her hair. It wasn't until she found herself on the road toward town, the brownies in her hands, that she allowed herself to realize she was on her way to Eric.

But the truth was, he'd nearly tripped down the steps in his haste to get away this morning—tripped like a gangly fourteen-year-old who suddenly couldn't think of anything to say. When he had first seen her, his eyes had filled with a hungry appreciation any woman that wasn't a complete idiot would recognize. It had pained her a little, and she knew she'd given him what her daddy would have called "a dirty look."

And then Eric, flustered, had turned to flee, nearly tripping on the stairs. It made him seem so vulnerable that Celia had been thinking about him all day. As old-fashioned as it was, she was taking him brownies to make up for being mean.

Thick evening fell, turning the sky a purply silver above the cottonwoods and pines as she walked. Hidden just beyond her field of vision, Jezebel sang softly to the gathered birds drinking from her skirts. Aside from the chiming of crickets and the occasional call of a bird, the world along this narrow country road was still.

Celia found herself slowing, feeling every pore in her body open to the warm, cottony air, to the nectar of silence no city could ever hope to reproduce. As it had so many times since she'd finally accomplished her dream of coming here, a swell of joy overtook her.

Never before had she felt as if a place embraced her, as if the land itself welcomed her into its bosom. Only in Gideon.

Home at last.

She had never been to Laura Putman's house, but a discreet inquiry at the grocery store had narrowed it down to only three possibilities. She passed the first with a wave to an old man who smoked a pungent pipe. He nodded and puffed.

As she approached the second house, several hundred yards farther on, she heard the mournful notes of a harmonica floating in the air. Her nerves rustled. She knew the sound of a harmonica would now always remind her of Eric.

She slowed her steps even more, listening. The notes were poignantly sad. They conjured up slow marches through rainy graveyards and widows cloaked in black and something even deeper and wider and more sorrowful yet. It pierced her clear through.

The house was an older bungalow, in need of paint but otherwise sound. As Celia turned up the swept path, she saw Eric. He sat in a kitchen chair on the wooden porch, shirtless and barefoot in the warm evening. When he spied her, he played two or three more notes, watching her come up the path, then put the harmonica down.

She climbed the steps in his silence, and when it was clear he wouldn't speak, she held out the brownies. "I brought you something."

He eyed the plate, then took it from her carefully, a little shyly. "Thank you."

His hair gleamed with a fresh washing, falling in casual disarray around his face and neck in glossy black waves. A single curl rested against the rise of a muscle in his shoulder and Celia resisted the urge to smooth it back into place.

"Have any luck finding your sister?" she asked.

"No." The word was nearly a growl.

Celia saw his throat move as he swallowed his worry. All locked up tight behind the walls, she thought. Impulsively, she reached forward to touch his arm. "It'll be okay, Eric."

At her touch, he flinched, then yanked his arm away in an almost violent gesture. "Go home and leave me be, would you?"

Her first instinct was to whirl around and do exactly that. Let him brood alone. But that was pride speaking. Another part of her, one she didn't dare put a name to, saw how frightened he was.

She knelt next to his chair. He kept his head bent, as if refusing to look at her would make her disappear. Celia simply waited, absorbing some of the terror that seeped from behind the walls.

After a few minutes, a little of the fight left him. His shoulders eased, and he touched the brownies on the plate with one finger.

Celia lifted her head to the crook of his elbow. His jaw tightened, and he didn't move. His gaze was fixed firmly on the brownies. He needed conversation, the ordinary give and take. It didn't matter what she said, only that she gave him a chance to let go of some of that worry.

"You know," she began, "when you showed up on my doorstep in that storm, I was really afraid you were a serial killer or something."

He glanced at her quickly, a smile flickering momentarily over his lips before he could wipe it away.

Encouraged, Celia settled next to him more comfortably. "On my way here, I was thinking that I love this place. I wish more than anything that I could have grown up here."

"If you had, you wouldn't be here now," he said. All at once, he leaned back in his chair and flipped the thin plastic film covering the brownies. "How'd you know I have a weakness for caramel and pecans?"

Celia shrugged. "I didn't," she admitted. "Tell me what it was like when you were a child."

He mulled the question, chewing with obvious enjoyment. "Wasn't a whole lot different, I guess. The people are a little bit better educated now, maybe, but not much."

Darkness had fallen. Eric said, "Why don't you hop up and turn on the porch light? Switch is just inside the door."

Celia did as he asked, but nothing happened.

He gave her a rueful smile. "I forgot."

"Me, too." With a shrug, she settled back onto the porch railing. Their knees were inches apart. "How much longer before they get the electricity back on?"

"Won't be long now." He licked caramel from his thumb and extended the plate. "Have one. You're a good cook, Celia."

"Thanks." She leaned forward to take a brownie. "Where are your parents, Eric? You talk about your sister, but never them."

He took his time choosing another brownie from the plate and picked a pecan half from the top before he spoke. "I never knew my daddy," he said at last. "Don't even know who he was. Laura tried to find out a few years ago, but nobody would talk. Mama never married him."

Celia didn't know exactly how old he was, but she'd guess his age to be thirty or a little more. Back in the days of his early childhood, women did not bear children out of wedlock, especially not in small towns. "That must have been hard for her."

A soft smile touched his mouth. "No, she didn't care what they thought. I think she really loved my father, whoever he was, and figured if she couldn't have him, at least she'd have us."

"So where is she now?"

"Last time Jezebel threw a temper tantrum, she took my mother with her." He set the plate of brownies aside. "I was six years old, and the house we lived in was down there on the other side of the river. It always flooded a little every spring, but that year, it just didn't stop raining."

Celia remembered the expression of dread that had crossed his face sometimes as he viewed the destruction wrought by the flood. "You were only six?"

"Mama pushed me and Laura up on the roof and we hung on for hours and hours and hours. She was with us for a long time, singing and telling us to pray. And then, all of sudden, she was gone."

"Oh, Eric. I'm sorry."

"Seems silly when I think about it with my head, but you know, I never really have stopped missing her. With this flood and Laura gone, I've been thinking about her a lot."

A part of Celia was surprised at the tumble of words spilling from him, and yet it was exactly what she'd hoped for. "What was she like?"

Eric shifted, picked up his harmonica and fiddled with it. "She was pretty," he said. "And she liked singing. A long time ago, she sang sometimes at the Five O'Nine, at a time when white women didn't do that much."

"She must have been brave."

"Stubborn, more like." He grinned and gave Celia a rueful lift of the eyebrows. "Runs in the family."

She smiled in return. "That should give you some faith in finding your sister."

He took a breath and blew it out, then touched the bridge of his nose for an instant. "Well, it does and it doesn't. I don't know why the hell she'd leave this house when she knew the river was rising. It doesn't make any sense."

"Do you have other family here?"

"An uncle. We lived with him after Mama died, but he's an old drunk—Laura wouldn't have bothered with him. He's a mean old son of a—" He inclined his head. "Sorry."

"I've heard a swear word or two in my life." A clear picture of his life was emerging. The child of a mother who would have been unkindly regarded, orphaned and sent into the care of an uncle who cared little for him.

Celia reached out to take one of Eric's scarred hands in her own. "No wonder you like my daddy's books. They're written about your life, aren't they?"

He looked up sharply, his eyes nearly black in the shadowy light. For a long, long moment, he simply stared at her, his hand loose in her own, his expression hard and unreadable. The hollows below his cheekbones gave him a hungry look, and Celia reached out with her other hand to touch the darkness on his face, hoping to somehow erase it.

Still his gaze didn't waver. Celia heard his call for her, a call coming from someplace deep inside of him. She leaned forward, surprised at her boldness, and for the second time, she kissed him.

This time she felt no surprise. His mouth met hers halfway, and it shocked her again with its tenderness. He tasted of chocolate and tea and midnight. It was all too easy to fall into that taste. She traced the corners and edges of his lips with her tongue and let her fingers fan open upon the planes of his face. At his jaw, there were tiny shifts as he moved to open his mouth, and against her index finger, his lashes swept down.

After a moment, he made a low, dark sound and swept Celia from her awkward perch into his lap. His fingers threaded through her hair. "Celia," he whispered against her mouth, "you're so sweet you're driving me crazy."

And then he kissed her again, thoroughly and deeply, leaving no doubt in Celia's mind about his area of expertise. His naked chest met her fingers, and she sighed at the silky, supple feel of his flesh under her palms. She explored the rise of muscles and the length of his upper arm, moved toward his neck and hair and explored them, as well. And all the while, Eric kissed her as if he could not drink deeply enough, as if the brush of their tongues and the press of their mouths were all that anchored him to life.

After a time he lifted his head and looked at her, looked hard into her eyes, and with one hand, he traced the curve of her cheek, the line of her jaw, the swell of her lip. He shook his head infinitesimally. "I've never met anybody like you, Celia." He swallowed, and his hand slipped into her hair, smoothing it away from her forehead. Beneath her, his legs were hard, and against her hand, his heartbeat rushed. "I'm not much of a talker, but you'd never believe that when I'm with you."

A wave of tenderness washed through her, and she buried her hands in his hair. It was thick and cool and smelled of shampoo. She leaned forward to rub it over her face, and as she did so, Celia felt Eric's mouth fall into the hollow of her throat.

It was searingly unexpected. She stiffened at the instant, urgent bloom of her nerves. "Eric," she whispered.

"I know," he murmured, his voice rumbling through his chest into hers. He planted a trail of kisses over her neck, and his hands moved with sudden purpose. "I know you think I oughta quit." He suckled hard at a spot just below her ear and a shimmer of sensation rocketed through her limbs. "Is that what you were gonna tell me?"

His drawl had slowed to a raw, dark-molasses rhythm. "You gonna tell me to stop, sugar?" His fingers teased the sides of her breasts and skittered away as his mouth slid along her jaw, as moist and slow as his voice.

Celia had no words. Her body was curiously taut and limp all at once, and she clutched his shoulders urgently, needing to somehow return his touch.

As his hand teased back to her breast, skimming over the aroused tip to the square, loose neckline of her sundress, Celia shifted against him and settled her mouth on his neck. She imitated the movements he had made, drawing circles with her tongue over his throat and suckling his earlobe and biting lightly at his jaw.

Where he'd been teasing and controlled, now he grew urgent. He tipped up her chin roughly to take his kiss and she could feel the hard thrust of his tongue. Against her hip, his erection was fierce and hot, and he moved against her almost unconsciously as he covered her breast with his hand, stroking restlessly through the cloth. A soft, deep noise rumbled through his chest.

Urgently, he pushed the strap of her dress from her shoulder and slid the fabric from her flesh. When his fingers plucked the bared tip, an electric shimmer bolted through her. She gasped aloud, clutching at him.

His mouth slipped over her jaw, over her throat and the swell of her breast. He uttered her name in a ragged voice.

Celia thanked the darkness that covered them, thanked the moonless sky as she helplessly let her head drop back against the crook of his elbow and felt his mouth fall on her breast to tug with feverish pressure at her nipple. A wildness built within her and she moved against him restlessly, grasping his silky big head in her hands, whimpering softly into the thick night.

And as if he could not get enough, he lifted her back to him, pressed her bared breasts against his naked chest and took her mouth with bruising, wild intensity. Celia could not think for the shimmering in her limbs, the heat pooling between her legs and deep in her belly as his tongue thrust and slid between her lips and over her tongue. His hands gripped her back and held her hard against the rigidness of his hunger.

She thought if a person could die of pleasure, she'd be dead ten times.

Who cared if he walked away? How many times did a woman have a chance to make love with a man like this, a man who looked like he ought to be on a record cover or in an ad for a motorcycle?

And not only that. He needed her—she could feel it. Not just physically, but in the very heart of him. It was his soul that urged her closer, urged her to kiss him, urged her now to move against him in greater invitation, move her breasts against his chest to make him moan softly, move her hips against his rigidness to make him clutch at her fanny.

All at once, Eric grabbed her tight and pressed her head into his shoulder. Celia felt the same trembling in his limbs she'd felt the day he left the farmhouse. It shivered in his arms and legs and deep in his chest. He held her so hard against him that she could barely breathe. His jaw was pressed into her forehead, his arms wrapped all the way around her.

"Lord have mercy," he whispered.

Celia tried to move, about to answer him, but he kept her pressed to him so tightly, she felt a sheen of sweat break on their flesh, across her back where his forearms rested, on her arms where his wrists bent around her, against her breasts where they pressed against his ribs.

Slowly the ferocity of passion passed. The whirring roar of noise in her ears quieted until she could hear his breath and the rhythmic chirp of crickets in the bushes and the slowing of his heart against her body. The trembling in his limbs eased, and with it came a loosening of his hold on her. Gently, he pulled her dress back into place.

His words, when they came, shocked her. "Celia," he said in a ragged voice, "please go."

A rigidness had crept into his body. Celia stood up, puzzled. "Eric—" she began.

He cut her off, his dark head bent. "Please, Celia."

So without a word, she turned and went down the stairs, walking into the night without fear, leaving Eric Putman behind on his porch.

By the time she reached the farmhouse, her calm had broken, and she sank down on the steps to bury her head in her arms. Her body ached with the lingering traces of his lips and hands, and her breasts were heavy with unfulfilled need.

Once or twice in her life she'd been infatuated. As a teenager, she'd spun endless fantasies about an Austrian boy who had helped in the gardens. In college, there had been a long-term but rather hollow alliance with a fellow teaching student. She'd often dreamed of finding the kind of passionate relationship her parents had shared, a passion so deep, it barely left room for children.

The instant Eric had walked through her door, she'd known he was the kind of man who could awaken her in that way. She hadn't expected she would awaken him in return.

Now she didn't quite know what to do. She didn't know what would happen if she gave in to that passion with Eric, didn't know how she would feel when his restless feet carried him away from Gideon again.

A wave of hunger clutched her middle as she thought of his fiercely demanding touch. Maybe it would be worth it. Maybe this was her only chance to know what it was like to be carried away on a tide of overwhelming sexual passion. Maybe once she found out what it was like, she could settle in and find that farmer who'd be content to raise his children in Gideon.

She swallowed in fear and with heady anticipation; fear because she might just find herself burned completely raw in that fire; anticipation because she knew it was too late to draw back now. It had been too late the minute he had appeared on her porch in the storm.

Chapter Eight

Eric awakened the next morning to the call of a noisy magpie in the tree outside his window. A jay joined in the squabble, which was then augmented by the chittering of a squirrel. At last came the reason for their noise: a long, annoyed meow.

He shifted, untangling himself from the sheets. Bright, golden sunlight streamed into the room as he slipped into a pair of jeans and wandered out onto the porch.

Sauntering down the road, his tail in the air, was the neighbor's cat. The jay trailed behind, hopping from tree to tree to scream warnings to hapless mice and sparrows about the monster in their midst. The cat paused and swiveling his big head, glared at the bird with fierce and sleepy green eyes. His tail twitched dangerously. The blue jay sat on its perch for a moment, shrieking, then with a flap of wings, headed for safer ground. The cat, obviously satisfied, settled on the edge of the road to lick his paws.

Eric leaned on the porch rail, grinning, and even that small act pleased him, because for the first time, the cut on his lip didn't split and bleed.

With a small, warm jolt he realized all the tight muscles in his shoulders had eased. His chest, so full of hollow worry the past week, felt normal. Even the morning seemed full of hope.

He would know if Laura were dead. He would just know. In the serenity of the gentle morning, he knew she was alive—not where she was or why she'd left her safe house here in the woods, but he'd find that out.

Yesterday he'd called every hospital and doctor's office and sheriff's office in the three-county stretch of the flood, and no one had seen anybody even faintly resembling his sister. The only thing he could do now was wait.

And in front of him stretched a fine summer day with nothing to do. He smiled and thought of a little spot on the river.

His supplies had been depleted with the storm, and worry over Laura had kept him from replacing them. Eric walked the mile into town, fishing pole slung over his shoulder, his empty backpack in his hand. As he walked, he found himself whistling in good humor.

Even the old buildings of Gideon's six-block downtown looked good to him. He stopped at the Piggly-Wiggly to buy some apples and hot dogs, Oreos and soda. The girl behind the counter smiled shyly at him, and Eric found himself flirting easily, chuckling to himself at the blush on her teenage cheeks.

A woman pushed her cart into his legs, gently but insistently. "Eric Putman, you incorrigible flirt, leave that poor girl alone and let me get my groceries."

Eric turned with a laugh to see Mrs. Greer, who'd been his Sunday school teacher for more years than he could count. He chuckled. "Can't teach an old dog new tricks," he said.

She pushed at her basket again, backing him up out of the way. "You always were too good-lookin'. Now you think because you went out and got yourself famous, the girls will all swoon for you."

Eric laughed, holding up a palm in defense. "I swear, I wasn't doing anything!"

"When are you gonna settle down and get married anyway?" she asked with a hand on her hip. "We need some more Putman children to liven up this old town."

He winked at the cashier and gave her a bill to pay for his small cache of food. "Well, Miz Greer," he drawled, "you're already married, and this pretty lady's got a big old diamond on her finger, so I guess I'm out of luck."

Mrs. Greer shook her head with a smile. "I'd sure like to see you hang around here, honey. Gideon needs its young."

He gave her a mock bow. "I'll give it some thought."

"You do that." She plopped a bag of oranges onto the conveyor belt. "You have any more records coming out that I should know about?"

He paused. She knew as well as anyone else in town that he wasn't making music these days, but she never said anything without a reason. His mouth came up with an answer his head knew nothing about. "I've been working on a few things," his mouth said, and his eye winked. "I'll let you know."

Mrs. Greer nodded. As Eric pushed out the door, he heard the cashier whisper loudly, "That was Eric Putman? Oh, my God! My fiancé's gonna go crazy when he hears."

Out on the sidewalk, Eric smiled to himself, feeling the same heady thrill he always felt when somebody he had never seen or spoken to knew about his work. Mainly what he felt was amazed. Delighted. How could anybody help it? Here in Gideon, it always meant that much more because it was vindication, not only for himself, but for his mother and his sister. Maybe even his unknown father.

He strolled past the diner and the hardware store and the drugstore, remembering little trips to each as a child, to spend money he earned mowing lawns. With a quirk of his lips, he realized there were things about Gideon he missed—not all the time, not with all of his heart and soul, but with a kind of sad aching that struck him at odd times. He knew every square inch of the land here, knew the rhythms of the way people walked and where to find what.

He knew the names of the people who stopped to chat with him politely. He knew who'd be behind the

counter pouring coffee in the diner, who would sell
him nails in the hardware store. He knew that when he
stopped into the bait shop, Joe Terrell with his bald
head and impressive paunch would be dressed in a
striped work shirt and plain blue cotton pants that
slipped down too far.

And when it was Joe Terrell in the shop, balder and
paunchier than ever, Eric grinned. "Hey, Joe."

"Why, hello there, Eric." Joe straightened and
tugged at the waistband of his pants. "How the hell
are you, boy?"

"Not bad." He nodded. "Be a lot better when I can
get my line in the water."

Joe pursed his lips and gathered the supplies Eric
wanted—worms and hooks. Eric paid and wandered
out again, replete with his plans for the day.

And there across the street was Celia, nibbling a
doughnut as she admired a fall of cloth in a window.
Her fine hair glittered around her face in the early
sunshine. She wore a tank top over jean shorts that left
her long, long legs bare, and he was surprised to note
that she showed signs of tanning, rather than sport-
ing the burn he'd imagine the sun would give her.

It was almost as if he'd been expecting to meet her
out in the street. As he admired her slim, graceful
body, he realized it had been the time spent with Celia
in his arms last night that had given him this new op-
timism. It had been the comfort of her mouth on his
that had eased him enough to sleep well for the first
time since finding Laura's house empty. It had been
talking and talking and talking that had eased his hollow heart.

And in spite of pushing her away last night, he couldn't resist crossing the street this morning. He came up behind her. "Hey, sugar," he said close to her ear.

Her gaze met his in the reflection caught by the plate-glass window, then she turned, her gray eyes shimmering like river water at twilight. "Hi," she said openly.

He grinned. "What're you doing out so early this morning?"

"Escaping," she replied with a smile. "That attic is like a sauna." She bit into her doughnut with obvious pleasure and chewed it slowly. "And I'm so sick of cleaning, I just couldn't face another day of it."

So pretty, he thought, staring into her wide eyes. He wanted to kiss her right there in the street, but he didn't. "I'm running away, too. You like to fish?"

She frowned. "I doubt it. Don't you have to stab a worm to death to catch a fish?"

He laughed and felt the sound move through his chest like a miracle, breaking up the last lingering traces of worry. "Yep," he said. "But you also get to sit on the side of the river and eat and watch the birds and listen to Jezebel sing."

"Hmm." Celia smiled, and he could see that she was waiting.

"Come on," he said, and surprised himself by taking her hand. It was small and cool against his own and a fleeting memory of her massaging his aching hands in the middle of the night crossed his mind. "Let me show you my Gideon," he coaxed.

She nodded. "I hope you have the food. All I've got is two more doughnuts, and that won't be enough."

"I'll feed you," he promised, then bumped her teasingly with his shoulder. "For a little thing, you sure can eat."

"I know. Can't help it." She licked her finger cheerfully. "I'm sure I'll be a round old woman, just like my grandmother."

"You don't care?"

She smiled. "No. There are much worse things than being a soft pillow for grandchildren."

"So you plan on having children, do you?"

"Yes—many, so that they have lots of brothers and sisters, and then—" she smiled up at him with a touch of whimsy "—I'll have about thirty grandchildren running around."

It was a peaceful, old-fashioned fantasy, and Eric was oddly touched. He gave her a sideways smile. "If those brownies are any indication, you'll be good at it."

Her silvery eyes met his steadily. "I know."

As if there was some magic that sprung from those fey eyes, he felt a silver ribbon spiral through him, bringing to life long-dead cells and byways, and blowing a cleansing wind through his dusty mind. For one tiny instant, he thought of her swelled big with his child.

His feet had slowed on the sidewalk as he stared into her face, alive with dreams he'd never ever entertained.

He grinned. "Come on. Fish'll be gone if we don't get down there."

* * *

It was a glorious day, Celia thought later, stretched out sleepily on a blanket in the grass by the river. She would never have dared explore Jezebel on her own, but with Eric along, pointing out paths and steering her around pitfalls, she felt safe. There were still more bugs flying and crawling and buzzing around than she'd ever dreamed existed, but Eric knew all their names and told her which ones to worry about. Mud daubers were big, black flying bugs that really hurt when they stung, but they didn't sting very often. Tics were tiny black or brown bugs with hard shells and they didn't hurt, but if you spent time outside, you had to remember to check yourself over for them. The rest were ordinary and irritating, but not dangerous—mosquitoes and horseflies and ants. It somehow made the environment seem less threatening to know what was what.

Twice Celia saw snakes glide by in the water, slipping into stands of cattails. A snapping turtle once grabbed Eric's line, getting a hook stuck in his lip. Eric, cursing, freed the creature and moved a few feet upriver to avoid him.

Eric. She crossed her arms on her knees and propped her chin on her wrists, looking at him. This Eric, with his dancing eyes and quick grin and teasing asides, had been glimmering below the surface since she'd met him, but this was the first time he'd allowed that side of him to show.

He stood at the edge of the river, shirtless and barefoot, which seemed to be the mode of dress he preferred. As she admired the taut lines of his smooth back, she remembered how sleek that burnished flesh had been against her palms last night.

As if he felt her gaze, he turned and gave her a wink. "Getting bored?"

She simply shook her head. It was as natural to admire him in the sleepy heat of high noon as it was to slip off her shoes in the evenings.

He smiled and propped his fishing pole beneath two rocks, then ambled over to sit beside her. The warmth of his sculpted arm radiated outward to touch her, and she lazily smiled.

All day she'd been waiting. Waiting for him to reach out to kiss her, touch her. Something.

He'd held her hand, nudged her with his elbow, squeezed her shoulder. Nothing more.

Now he plucked a long strand of grass with a bushy end and leaning on one elbow, reached up to tickle her nose with it. "How do you like my Gideon?"

"I like it," she said, brushing the grass away. "It's so peaceful you can cut it with a knife."

"Knives aren't very peaceful," he said with a chuckle.

As he looked at her, his blue eyes sparkled with something akin to happiness. "You know what I mean," she said.

"Yeah." He dropped the blade of grass and fell backward onto the blanket, grabbing her hand.

Celia leaned over him. "If I didn't know better, I'd say you were actually happy right at this moment."

He opened his eyes and lifted a devilish eyebrow. "I've got another word for it," he drawled.

She tilted her chin upward. "No, you don't. It's just been so long you forgot what to call it."

Slowly, he licked his full bottom lip, his eyes dancing. "*Randy* is the word I was thinking of."

Celia smiled, and that, too, was natural. She felt as though she'd known him always, since birth. It was that easy to be with him. All day he'd talked to her about Gideon and his time on the road. He'd told her stories about getting caught in a biker bar once in Chicago and talking to the wrong woman; about tripping and falling off a stage in New Orleans, right into the lap of a fat woman who instantly grabbed him; about his sister finding a tutu she wore around the house for months when she was nine. He made Celia laugh until her cheeks hurt from smiling.

In turn, she told him about her parents accidentally leaving her behind in a Brussels train station; about the time her mother decked a photographer in a Milan restaurant; about girls in boarding school.

So now it was easy to lean close and put a hand on his chest. "Randy?" she repeated. "Unless I've got my slang mixed up, that means, er, lusty?"

Still grinning, he nodded.

"Why didn't you say so sooner?" she asked, and since he didn't seem like he'd mind and she was tired of waiting, she kissed him. It was gentle and warm, and she released him after a moment.

His mouth had softened with her kiss, but the gentle shine didn't flee from his eyes. Instead he lifted one hand and touched her cheek. "Maybe it is just happy," he said in his low, dark voice.

Celia took one big hand into both of hers. With a light touch, she explored the long graceful lines, admiring the strength and size and elegance of a hand designed to create. The thready scars, white against the darkness of his flesh, seemed a sacrilege—and all at once she knew they also held the key to the loneliness that clung to him like perfume. "What happened to your hands, Eric?"

He pursed his lips. His eyes sobered and Celia knew she'd hit the mark. With a small, slow sigh, he lifted his free hand, examining it as if it belonged to someone else. "I used to play guitar," he said quietly. "I miss it so much sometimes...." His voice trailed off as he flexed his fingers.

Celia inclined her head, waiting. She'd learned that his stories came out slowly, in their own way, end to beginning as often as beginning to end.

He sat up. "I left home when I was sixteen. Laura had gone to Dallas for cosmetology school, and I didn't want to hang around here without her, so I took my guitar and my harp and hitchhiked to New Orleans." He picked up a stick that he used to draw in the dirt at his feet. "It took some time, but I really did make a name for myself out there with my songs."

The story rumbled out in his ragged, dark voice. He spoke quietly, but even the insects seemed to have gone silent to hear.

"About five years ago, I came back to Gideon for a visit and somehow or another when I left, I had a woman with me. Her name was Retta Neely, and her family was the only one in town with a worse reputation than my own. I guess I felt sorry for her."

He cleared his throat and looked at Celia. "That's a lie." A faint gleam of sardonic amusement twisted his lips. "She was the kind of woman I thought I wanted at the time. Fast and sexy and wild."

Celia tried to swallow a smile, but before she wiped it completely away, he caught it. "If you laugh at me, Celia Moon, all they'll find left of you is little pieces in the woods."

She laughed outright, then at his expression of utter bewilderment, she smoothed the corners of her lips with her fingers. "Sorry. Go ahead."

"It's a sad story, Celia."

"I know. I'm sorry."

A glimmer of amusement sparked in his dark blue eyes, and he smacked her ankle lightly. "Hush now."

Celia nodded and tucked her tongue over her teeth to sober herself.

"*Anyway,*" he said pointedly, "we were okay for a couple of years. Sometimes she drank too much and got pretty crazy, but I understood that she just didn't know that she had anything." He frowned, then glanced at Celia, looking for understanding. "All she thought she had was her body, you know? She didn't know she..."

He shook his head. "Anyway. The drinking got a little worse and little worse, and nothing I did or said made her feel any better."

Celia thought of her mother. "I know people like that."

He glanced at her and a light dawned in his eyes. "Yeah, I bet you do."

She raised her eyebrows but didn't speak.

"Well," he continued, clearing his throat. "I didn't know it at the time, but she started having an affair or whatever you want to call it with one of the guys in the band. I didn't find out until it'd been going on for about six or eight months.

"We were playing a club in Charlotte for a couple of weeks. It was big deal, a lot of money and exposure. And the longer we were there, the worse Retta got. One night while I was playing, she started booing us."

Celia winced.

"Yeah." Eric inclined his head. "It was pretty bad. A bouncer finally got her outside, but she was waiting in the alley when we came out. She was so drunk she could hardly stand up, and she started yelling at me and this other guy, the one she'd been sleeping with."

Eric rubbed his face. "Why am I telling you this?"

"Because I asked."

He jumped up, crossed to his fishing pole and adjusted it minutely, then turned around, his hands on his hips. For a moment Celia didn't know if he would go on. He looked at her hard, then returned to her side.

"I lost it—just finally lost it. I'd felt sorry for her and tried to help her as much as I could, but she was so nasty that night, I just lost my temper." He paused, staring off over the river. "I loaded her in the car. She was screaming filthy words at me and the band, acting the fool. I told her if she wanted to be a fool, she could do it at home in Gideon where I didn't have to put up with it. I was going to drive her to the airport.''

Celia reached for his hand and pressed it between her own. A shimmer of sunlight glossed his black hair as he bent his head.

''It was raining, the middle of the night—I was furious with Retta, but nothing like she was at me. It was crazy. The whole time I drove, she screamed and slapped me, scratched my face—'' He broke off, and his jaw went rigid. ''I hated her, Celia. I stomped on the gas pedal, trying to make her shut up.'' He swallowed, and when he resumed speaking, his tone of voice was flat and hard. ''I lost control of the car. We slammed into a tree going about ninety. I went through the windshield. Retta didn't go anywhere.''

''Eric,'' she said softly.

''No.'' He tugged his hand from Celia's and stood up. ''You haven't heard the worst of it. When I woke up in the hospital, I didn't even care that she was dead. All I cared about was my hands and if I could play guitar.''

The dark loneliness filled his eyes again and Celia regretted her impulse to ask about his hands. All the joy of the day had been wiped away—at least for him. She'd chased him back into the shadows with her question.

She stood up and touched his back. He flinched. Celia closed her eyes, then leaned against him, pressing her forehead into the smooth flesh of his shoulder blade. ''I'm sorry, Eric. It was none of my business and I shouldn't have asked.''

A small, strangled noise came from him, and he lifted one arm, then let it drop. "I wish I could forget it, but it's gonna be on my conscience forever. Because of me, Retta's dead. Every time I look at my hands, I remember that I killed her."

Celia lifted her head and rounded his tall frame to look at him. Guilt was seamed into the grim lines of his face. She touched the hard planes with her fingers, using both hands to try to smooth the sorrow. "So you keep running."

He grabbed her arms above the elbow, grabbed them fiercely. "You keep looking at me with that hero look in your eyes, Celia, and I keep trying to tell you that I'm not the man you think I am."

"You aren't the man *you* think you are, either." She didn't pull away, in spite of the boiling glimmer in his eyes. "I've never seen anyone who was as hard on himself as you are."

His eyes narrowed. "You don't get it. I'm the bastard child of a woman everyone in this town had a name for. I've never had anything to call my own, and for most of my life I rarely had two nickels to rub together. I dropped out of high school when I was sixteen and never went back. The only thing in the world I had was that guitar and now that's gone, too. I don't have anything to give you."

Oh Eric, don't you see what you have?

She wanted to touch his mouth, set in such hard lines, but in his present mood he might bite her fingers off. The thought made her nearly smile again, but this time she caught it before any of it showed.

She put her hand flat on his chest and waited until she could feel the heavy thud of his heart against her palm. "Your heart," she said, and looked at him.

Puzzlement chased away some of the fury in his eyes.

"Your heart's broken," she said softly. "That's all that's wrong with you."

He rolled his eyes, exasperated. "Celia—"

"No. It's your turn to listen to me." Keeping her hand pressed against the life-sustaining heat of his heart, she said, "You'd like me to believe that you took Retta with you because she was good in bed and that was it. But the truth is, you don't have a mean bone in your body. Another man might take on a woman for the sake of sex, but I've got a feeling you really did feel sorry for Retta, and you did what you could to give her a break." She smiled with a little shrug. "Which isn't to say you didn't enjoy her, uh, company."

She stood on her tiptoes to press a kiss to his beautiful mouth. "Whenever you get over feeling sorry for yourself, you know where I am."

As she walked away from him, Celia felt her own heart pounding. Her mouth had opened of its own accord, and maybe she'd been wrong. She hesitated, then turned around.

Eric stood at the edge of the river, his head bent into his hand. His bare feet were planted in the mud, and his other hand was braced on his hip. His pain radiated from him like steam, almost visible in the hazy, humid air.

What he needed was to be loved, deeply and completely and unconditionally. Not for his beauty or his talent or his sexy, sexy ways. Just because he was Eric Putman, unique in all the world.

The problem was she kept getting tangled in her own past, in the scenarios torn from her father's stupid books and in fear. Fear that she might be falling in love with Eric. It terrified her that she could even consider such a thing, that she could fall victim to fate like that.

This morning, talking about babies and grandchildren, she'd put Eric in the role of daddy and grandpa. She'd offered her vision of the peaceful future to tempt him.

But his stories this afternoon had seemed especially designed to illustrate to her just how far his life was from the role she wanted to cast him in. Babies and grandchildren and long evenings on the porch? Fat chance.

As she stood there staring at him across a field of grass, with the sun burnishing his skin with gold, she wanted to weep. In spite of all her resolves, she was falling in love with him.

Furious now with both of them, she whirled and stomped away, walking along the banks of Jezebel, who had deposited him on her doorstep.

When Eric was firmly out of sight, she paused, breathing hard. "Why did it have to be *my* doorstep, Jezebel?" she asked the river. "There must be a woman that could handle him, but I'm not her."

She paused and realized she half expected the river to answer. Instead, Jezebel sang her own private song, rushing over rocks toward the place where Eric likely stood yet, lost in his own private hell.

Celia wavered, thinking of his posture as she'd left him. Maybe she ought to go back.

"No," she said aloud. "You comfort him, Jezzie. He's your son."

Chapter Nine

After Celia left him, Eric sank into a heap at the edge of the river. The cocoon of numbness he'd created for himself after the accident two years ago was crumbling fast.

It had started to crack when Celia had yanked her father's original manuscripts out of the trunk and thrown one at him. Excitement had shimmered all the way through him over those damned manuscripts.

That had been the first crack. Celia, with her wide-open kiss, had levered the split into a fissure.

From there, it had been disintegrating further each day. His sister's disappearance, being in the blues club and hearing his song, dancing with Celia—all had taken their toll. Last night when he'd begged her to go home before he'd lost control, he'd known there wasn't much left of his peace of mind.

Now he knew it was gone. He felt as rawly exposed as a half-formed moth.

In a black humor, he headed home. He checked the message machine, finding nothing. After dinner, he showered off the fishing trip from his body, and unable to bear the thought of another lonely evening in his sister's house, set out on foot for the Five O'Nine. If he was blown open, he might as well go where he was known.

It was early. The sun hadn't even set, but this was the time of day he had always walked over to the club when he worked there, and it felt natural. A handful of cars rested in the shade of a cottonwood tree, and the door was propped open to any wind that might stray from the river. As Eric crunched over the gravel of the lot, he heard a laugh ring out, and he knew someone had dropped some coins into the jukebox, because a tinny recording of Lightnin' Hopkins swirled suddenly into the evening.

Long, gold fingers of sunlight arrowed through the trees and fell through the open door, and as if they were the yellow-brick road, Eric followed them inside.

He paused a minute to let his eyes adjust to the dimness within. At the bar was a cluster of older men, some dressed in the ties they'd worn to work, others in field clothes. At this hour, the customers were mostly widowed or divorced old men looking for a little conversation before they returned to the quiet of their rooms. There was a younger couple in the corner, murmuring quietly between themselves, and a pair of young men played a game of pool, but most of the younger crowd would filter in later. There was something reassuring about the fact that the pattern hadn't changed.

He ambled toward the knot of drinkers at the bar. The bartender with the gold tooth looked up and grinned. "Hey, y'all," he said to the others at the bar, "look who's here."

The group turned as one, heads swiveling, and Eric slapped Wild Willie on the shoulder. "Hey, old man."

Willie grinned and gestured at the stool beside him. "Pull up a chair, boy, have a drink." He gestured to the bartender. "Just couldn't stay away, could you?"

Eric thought about lying, but he shook his head. "Nope."

"Well, you must've read my mind."

"Why's that? I know you don't have laryngitis."

Willie chuckled. "I might *get* it any minute, you don't behave." He leaned over the bar. "John, hand me that guitar."

Eric frowned as the bartender lifted a black case from a spot behind a case of beer. The light caught a scratch in the black leather that Eric recognized. "Where the hell did you find it?" he asked as Willie deposited the case in his hands.

"Some old tramp brought it in a day or two ago, trying to get a few drinks in trade." The rheumy eyes settled on Eric hard. "Now I'm not a man for signs and superstitions—"

"Uh-huh," Eric said sarcastically.

Willie glanced over his shoulder at his cronies in mock disgust. "This younger generation got no respect a-tall." Shaking his head, he turned back to Eric. "Like I was saying, I'm not much of a man for signs and superstitions, but this here guitar showing up like that, right here, made even me think a bit."

Eric ran a hand over the leather, traced the scar on the case that he'd picked up in the fight in Chicago that he'd told Celia about this afternoon. He'd spent days cursing his choice to leave the guitar behind, and his fingers were just a hair unsteady as he flipped the lid open.

And there it was, his guitar, a blue '57 Stratocaster, silky and cold to the touch. He smiled and let go of a long breath, running his fingers over the frets, the almost womanly dips and swells along the edge. A ripple of relief washed through him, and he had a peculiar, powerful urge to hug it, kiss it, press it close against his chest. Instead, he just looked at Willie and raised his eyebrows.

"And you think you can turn your back on the blues," Willie said in a soft voice. "Boy, those teeth are sunk so deep in your heart, they ain't never gonna let you go."

Eric pursed his lips. He laughed without mirth. "I know, Willie," he said quietly. "I know."

"Why don't you hang around awhile? There's a boy comin' in who'd really like to meet you."

"Who is it?" Eric closed the case and eased it down to lean against the bar, close to his leg.

"Local fella. Name's James. He's gonna fill in for Cat tonight."

Eric nodded. "I'll be here."

Willie nodded and clapped him on his shoulder as he stood up. "I'm gonna go have Betty fix me something to eat. You want to join me?"

Eric lifted his head. He'd already eaten a light supper, but the thought of salty, heavy cooking as prepared by the woman who'd been making such meals for the clientele of the Five O'Nine for twenty years or so was more than he could resist. "What's she got tonight?" he asked.

"Catfish. I caught it myself."

Eric chuckled to himself at the irony, then stood up to join the old man.

The boy, James, was just that—no more than seventeen at the outside; and already as tall as Eric. He ambled over to the vinyl booth where Willie and Eric ate from heavy porcelain plates. To learn that he was painfully shy took no more than a glance.

His shirt was buttoned to the collar and tight around the gangly wrists, an odd sight for Eric, who'd forgotten boys in the country didn't wear leather or cut designs in their hair: their mamas would kill them. As he slid in next to Willie at the old man's invitation, James cast a shy glance toward Eric.

"How you doin', man?" Eric said, spearing the last of his fish.

"I'm okay." James's voice was a gentle tenor, his smile tentative.

Eric pushed his plate aside and leaned comfortably on the table. "Willie says you're filling in for Cat tonight. You must play a pretty mean sax."

"Yes, sir," James said. "Well, I mean, uh—" He glanced at Willie, who nodded. James sighed and met Eric's eyes directly. "My grandpa wanted me to play the sax and I'm okay, but I want to play blues guitar—I mean," he said, ducking his head momentarily, "I already play, but I want to play like you. I've heard you every time you been home and have two records you played on, and every record that anybody made with your songs." Earnestly, he gestured with his long-fingered dark hands. "I never heard anybody play guitar like you do—did." He gulped and fell back in the booth. "I'd be real honored if you'd teach me some of your licks. But if you don't want to, I mean, I understand. Willie told me..."

Despite himself, Eric grinned at Willie, who had a fond smile on his wide mouth. "He doesn't have a lot of trouble once he gets going, does he?" Eric asked.

Willie touched his nose with the pad of his thumb and chuckled. "Reminds me of somebody else I know."

Between Willie and Eric passed a hundred memories—a thousand—beginning with a spiel much like the one Eric had just heard.

Eric looked back to James's dark face, to his wide, earnest eyes, and he saw the hunger there—the hunger to somehow *be* the blues. He filled his lungs with air and blew it all out. "I don't know," he said slowly. "My hands..."

James tried to hide his crestfallen expression. He was unsuccessful. But bravely, he inclined his head and half shrugged. "I understand."

Quickly he got to his feet. "I gotta warm up."

Eric swore under his breath, watching the boy walk away. It seemed lately as though everything he did was wrong.

"You know," Willie said in his slow drawl, "ain't many boys his age want to play blues anymore. They all want to sing rap or play heavy metal." He growled the terms. "There's some who say the blues is dying. 'Less we all share what we know, your grandbabies won't never know it."

Eric looked up, but Willie had already slid from the booth. "I got some work to do myself," he said.

There's some who say the blues is dying. Over the next few hours, as Eric watched the crowd amble in, as he listened to the bluesmen on the small corner stage, the words echoed in his head over and over and over.

By the time the club had grown hot with bodies and smoky with cigarettes and friendly with drink, Eric made up his mind. A world without blues was not a world he wanted to live in. When the band took a break, he crossed the room and touched James's shoulder.

"Can you come to my sister's place tomorrow? Maybe about five?"

James smiled. "Yeah."

He held out a hand and Eric took it. "We'll see what we can do."

Old Wild Willie, standing nearby, nodded solemnly.

* * *

It was late. Celia knew she ought to get to bed, get some rest. Instead she sat on the porch, staring over the dark fields as if they could tell her what to do.

She was worn out. The house, in spite of long days of work, was still a mess. Most of the mud had been shoveled out, and she'd even made some progress in throwing out the ruined artifacts of her grandmother's life, but everything stank to high heaven.

The attic was stifling, even with a fan, and she didn't even want to *try* to sleep in this restless mood.

So now she sat on the porch with one of her father's books in hand, reading. She'd been going through the novels for several days, trying to decipher where his stories ended and the real Gideon began. Especially tonight, after her recent encounters with Eric, she felt the lines blurring.

She cursed her father softly, more sure than ever that she was unconsciously living out one of his dramas. And why? To bring him back somehow? To punish him for running away?

"Damn you, Daddy!" she cried aloud, and with a guttural noise, she threw the book as hard as she could into the dark yard. Then she buried her head in her arms, needing to cry. "I miss you," she whispered.

A soft swish in the grass made her lift her head. There, emerging like a specter from the darkness, was Eric. He carried a guitar case in one hand.

In spite of the way they had parted this afternoon, Celia felt no surprise at seeing him. He bent over to scoop up the book Celia had thrown, then quietly joined her on the steps. "There must be some kind of blues you could sing over your daddy,'' he said in his rough voice.

He smelled faintly of whiskey and heat. ''What are you doing out so late?'' Celia asked, wiping her cheeks dry.

''Been to the Five O'Nine.''

''Drowning your sorrows?''

''I had every intention of getting so drunk, somebody had to carry me home.'' He chuckled and leaned on the step behind him. ''The trouble is, I never have been able to develop a taste for real hard drinking.''

In spite of herself, Celia smiled. ''I won't tell anybody.''

''I'd appreciate that. Might completely ruin my image.''

He was just a little tight, as her grandmother used to say. A little bit friendlier than usual, a little more cheerful, a little less intimidating. As he handed Celia the book, he let his arm graze her leg, and he leaned a little closer yet.

In his rumbling voice, he asked, ''Why'd you throw it?''

''I don't know. I'm just so angry with him still.'' She took a breath, shaking her head. ''He knew that road like he knew keys on a typewriter. He could have driven it blindfolded.''

''So he killed himself.''

''Yes.'' The knowledge stung deeply.

''And it hurt your feelings that he wanted to get back to his wife more than he wanted to stay with you.

Celia jumped up. ''Yes! They never had time for me. They only cared about each other. I was an afterthought, always. I don't understand why they even bothered to have a child.''

''You really miss him.''

Celia nodded, feeling tears well in her eyes again. ''I really do.''

Eric smiled gently and held out one broad hand. ''Come here. Sit down.'' When she settled reluctantly next to him, he pulled the harmonica from his pocket. ''We'll just sing some blues,'' he said, and there was mischief in his eyes. '' 'Celia's Blues.' ''

She gave him a skeptical look.

He started to sing, obviously making up the song as he went along, about a wandering man named Jacob Moon. But he put a silly turn on the words and used his harp to make light, leaping notes. It made her laugh. When Eric saw that he was being successful, he got ever sillier, making up absurd rhymes and hitting high notes that were far beyond his reach.

Finally, Celia slapped his shoulder. ''Enough!'' She grinned at him. ''It helps,'' she pronounced. ''Now maybe you should sing one for your sister.''

He moistened his lip, looking at her, and even in the darkness, his eyes held a mystical blue color. All mirth fled his face. He bent his head over the harp and blew a soft, mournful cry of notes. A ripple passed through Celia's belly—a warning.

Then Eric opened his mouth and began to sing, really sing. The words told a story of loneliness and a long search for safe harbor, of a pretty woman abused by a world too harsh for her gentle ways.

It was a beautiful, sad, poetic song, but the words were insignificant in comparison to the voice that sang them.

His speaking voice was almost unbearably rich, dark, low and seductive; having heard it, Celia should have expected that he could sing like this. But as she listened, she realized, too, that she could never have known how beautiful it was without hearing it. He sang low and hard and with great power, the notes raspy here, clear there; so rich and deep, she ached with the power of it. His was a voice perfectly suited to singing blues ballads, and the longer he sang, the more she pulsed with it. Tears began to stream from her eyes unheeded as she thought of his sister and her father and Eric himself, aching for all of them. Aching for herself.

Eric finished the song, staring out toward the fields where lightning bugs sparked in the grass like fallen stars. His heart felt less heavy for having sung, and he sighed with deep satisfaction.

From beside him came Celia's voice, soft and filled with tears. "Eric," she whispered, "that was so beautiful."

He turned in surprise to see a wash of tears running over her pale cheeks. "Oh, sugar," he said, and without thinking, gathered her into his arms. Her fine hair splayed over his hand, and her face nestled into the hollow of his shoulder. Her arms slipped around him. "I didn't mean to make you cry," he said.

She felt like a fragile doll in his arms, so small that she might snap if he hugged her too tightly. But he'd learned that her fragility was an illusion, and he tugged her hard against him, feeling a well of emotion at the press of her damp face against his neck. She was vulnerable in ways, tender in others, but she was strong, and as he held her, he knew why he'd come.

"You should be singing, Eric," she said. "Your voice—"

"No," he whispered against her jaw, seeking her mouth. "I should be kissing you. I wanted to all day."

"I wanted you to." She lifted her head, her pale eyes full of trust and hunger. He bent his head and tasted her sweet lips, fitting his mouth over hers with ease. Such a soft mouth, he thought vaguely, drifting as she returned the kiss.

The simmering hunger he'd felt for her went up another notch, and forgetting that he'd sworn he would not give in to his passion, he traced the lines of her body with both hands—her long, slim back and the dip of her waist, the curve of her hip and thigh, even her calves. He tasted the flicker of her tongue against his and felt the edges of her pretty teeth. Her nose bumped his cheek and she made a small, low sound.

He lifted his mouth from hers, holding her head in his hand. Her eyes were slumberous, her mouth glistening with his kiss. The sight pushed his control beyond all recall. "I want you," he said raggedly, kissing her between words. With one hand he traced the line of her jaw, followed her neck and, staring into her eyes, cupped her breast, wondering again at the perfect nestling of it against his palm. "You make me feel like somebody else." He stroked the gentle rise of flesh and felt the pearling of the tip against his thumb. He settled his mouth over hers, pushing the fabric from her shoulders—first the loose blouse, then the plain, ordinary bra below. Her naked breast fell into his waiting hand and he heard her gasp and felt her try to pull away.

"I can't do this, Eric," she whispered. "Not if you're going to tell me you have to go. Don't make me go through another night like last night."

In answer, he bent his head to the soft skin in his palm and nudged the tip with his tongue, once, lightly, then settled his mouth over it, suckling at the heat. She made an airy, restless sound and grabbed his shoulders and he pushed her back against the post to brace her. He circled the incredibly soft, supple flesh of her breasts with his palms and tasted the column of her throat with his mouth, with his tongue.

"You're so beautiful, Celia," he said, lifting his head to look into her eyes, his fingers roving of their own accord over her. Her eyes grew sultry and her eyelids dropped, but she held his gaze without shyness or embarrassment as his hands moved over her. Slowly, looking at him, she lifted her hands to cover his and leaned forward to kiss him.

He exploded at the carnal thrust of her tongue and with a groan, he bent his head again to lick and suckle the rose-tipped rise of her breasts, lost in the taste of her satiny flesh, lost in the glory of Celia.

"Make love with me, Eric," she whispered. *With* her—not *to* her. Something swelled in his chest, and he growled low as he stood up, grasping her waist to pull her up with him. He kissed her at the door, pressing her into the threshold, his hands roaming her body as she clutched handfuls of his hair so tightly, it hurt him. She turned and backed them into the living room, her fingers freeing the buttons of his shirt as she walked.

At the foot of the stairs, he kissed her again, lost in his need for her. In an urgent need to feel her bared flesh, he pushed the tank top from her arms and chest into a pool at her waist, leaving her in that simple white bra, one strap falling down her arm. He tugged the clasps free and tossed it over his shoulder, taking her mouth as he let his hands roam the small, silky lines of her back, her slender shoulders, the fine round of her rib cage. Halfway up the stairs, they tripped together, but in spite of the jarring impact, they didn't lose touch. She pushed his shirt from his shoulders, her breath coming in hard, fast gasps. He felt the round give of her breasts against the wall of his chest and a jolt of electric sensation squeezed his heart. For an instant, he pressed her closer, reveling in the glory of her naked flesh against his own, and then he picked her up and carried her the rest of the way to the attic room where it had all begun.

Together they tumbled to the bed, kissing so wildly, Eric thought he would lose his mind before he could join with her completely.

And for the first time in his life, he felt a woman needed him as much as he needed her, for in Celia's kiss there were teeth, and her body arched in fierce hunger. She freed the buttons on his pants and pushed them away, and she restlessly stroked the curve of his naked buttocks and the backs of his thighs and the hollow of his spine, using her palms and fingers and nails.

Somehow in the madness, he found her completely bare below him, hot and shivering at once.

Only then did he pause, kneeling above her in the dark room, with moonlight pouring through the window. Her hair was as silvery as the light, and her big, gray eyes shone like captured moonbeams. He touched her breasts and her belly. "You're so beautiful, Celia. Like sugar."

She opened her arms to beckon him. "Eric."

Then he was lost, driving into the waiting heat of her, moving with urgent hunger and lost control. Celia met him, wrapping herself around him. It was not smooth or sweet; it was not elegant or polished. It was pure and elemental and primitive.

And yet as he held her and moved with her in the silence, his hands cupped around her bottom, his mouth against her neck, her arms flung hard around his shoulders, he felt a shock of joining that transcended anything he'd known. As they thrashed together, lost to anything but each other, he felt suddenly awash in a perfect silvery light, as if Celia had cloaked them with her magic. Where everything had been dark, now all glowed with light—a blazing, healing light he'd never seen, had never hoped to know. In Celia's arms he felt it in him to be all she saw in him, all the things he'd never dared dream of being.

And as their rhythm intensified, punctuated with breathless whispers and urgings and endearments and kisses, he felt tears. His own tears, running hot on his face. Ashamed, he bowed his head into her hair, feeling her tremble and shiver against him. She clutched his back and cried his name, and even as he tumbled into the very depths of her, his tears washed unchecked into the silk of her hair.

Lost, he thought, coming apart. He was so lost— and Celia felt like home.

Chapter Ten

As their breathing slowed, Celia felt a tingle moving through her body, spreading from the tips of her fingers and toes to radiate through her limbs and torso, through her organs and through her soul.

Eric's weight pressed her into the mattress, his powerful arms anchoring her even more tightly to him. His hair fell over her face, silky and cool. She flashed on their tangled, passionate ascent up the stairs and a bubble of laughter built in her chest. "Good grief," she said with a chuckle.

He lifted his head to look at her. There was a sheen of sweat over his brow, and a lock of black hair clung to the moisture on his cheek. "You laugh at the weirdest times."

The bubble chuckled over once more as she pushed his damp hair away from his hard jaw. "I think laughing when you feel good is perfectly appropriate."

The devilish expression flared in his eyes. "You feel pretty good, do you?" He moved against her and his nostrils flared.

She nodded slowly. "Mmm."

He kissed her, suddenly and urgently. "You taste like sunshine," he whispered, his big hand wrapped around her neck. "I can't remember the last time anything tasted as good as you do."

Again laughter swelled in her chest. "How about those brownies you ate in one sitting?"

"Not even those," he murmured, intently kissing her jaw.

Celia laughed and he let go of her. "What do you keep laughing about?"

"Quit scowling," she said, and rubbed her nose over the tip of his. "Not everything in life is that serious."

"This afternoon, that was a serious story and you giggled." His voice was puzzled, though, not angry.

"Eric, don't you see how melodramatic your whole life has been? It really is just like something my father would write. That's what has been driving me so crazy about you." She frowned at herself, wondering how she'd let that slip. With a distracted fascination, she touched the round of his shoulder, glorying in the satin sheen of his flesh, the supple feel of it against her palm. In the same mode, she bent and pressed first her lips, then her cheeks to the place.

The sound of his song for Laura whispered through Celia's mind. "You really should be singing, Eric." She lifted her head. "You have the most incredible voice I've ever heard."

"Thank you." A glitter of humor touched his eyes. "But I've got a feeling you're feeling just a teeny bit expansive at the moment."

"Do you ever accept a compliment?"

He mockingly frowned. "Try not to make a habit of it." He lifted an eyebrow. "Do you?"

"Why do I get the feeling we're getting off the subject here?"

"Are we?" With a quick movement, he pushed away the sheet Celia had demurely drawn up over herself, exposing her breasts to his gaze. In a rumbling voice, he asked, "What if I told you I think you have the prettiest breasts I've ever seen?"

Celia flushed as his hands and eyes roved over her. It was a flush of the spirit and one of the mind—she was embarrassed and pleased and suddenly, incredibly, aroused. Still, she strove for lightness. "I'd say it was sort of a backhanded compliment."

He paused, lifting his gaze in surprise. The beautiful lips were only millimeters away from hers. "Backhanded? Why?"

"Because it assumes you've seen quite a number of unclothed women."

"Mmm." He pushed her shoulders until she lay against the pillows. "I'm always giving backhanded compliments," he murmured against her lips. "But just because I'm clumsy when I open my mouth doesn't mean I don't mean it." As if to illustrate, he bent his head over her, taking one nipple into his mouth slowly. His hair fell forward to brush her flesh as his tongue swept silkily back and forth. "You really do have a pretty body," he whispered, and his breath added to the erotic sensations. His mouth slid lower, teasing over her ribs to her belly, where his tongue danced over her navel, sending a rocket of sensation through her. "Just right for my hands and my mouth, like they were made for me, waiting for me."

Her body rippled softly, but along with the response of her flesh, pleasurable but predictable, came a glow of acceptance. "Oh, Eric," she whispered, her hands tangling his hair.

"Women always want more than what they have," he said, and his mouth traveled down and up, over breasts and belly and arms. He kissed her mouth softly. "They want a smaller rear end and a skinnier waist and big breasts." He moved close to her, his naked body pressing along her side with heat and hard muscle and hair-dusted flesh. Celia swallowed, unable to prevent a small gasp.

"You're perfect, Celia." His fingers trailed lightly down the curve of her upper arm, tickling the sensitive inner crook of her elbow, to her hand. He lifted it gently, guiding her to the rigid evidence of how she pleased him. "You see?" he whispered.

With a sense of power and excitement, she let herself explore him, tentatively at first, then with greater abandon, trusting her instincts.

In turn, his hand slid over her belly, into the soft folds between her thighs, and his mouth settled again over the tips of her breast, teasing and dancing, his fingers sliding with exquisite pressure. She cried out at the overload of sensations and heard him growl as her fingers tightened around him.

All at once, he was poised above her, his legs pushing hers apart as he settled once again between them. His eyes were dark with passion, his color high in his cheeks, and as he paused at the threshold of their joining, he kissed her roughly. "You're not like anybody else, Celia."

Unable to bear the temptation, she arched to bring him home and heard their simultaneous cries an instant before she tumbled again into the explosive, erotic joy of loving Eric in a quiet void where they alone moved together.

The night was as enchanted as any fairy tale, Celia thought once, watching Eric laugh as she tickled his ribs and the bottoms of his feet. Enchanted because her sad drifter was happy when he made love to her; enchanted because kissing Celia made him forget that he could no longer play guitar. He made love the way he sang, slow and deep, and no matter how often he turned to her, Celia knew it would never be enough.

Toward morning, they dozed off. Eric held her close to him, as if she were an anchor, he a ship that would drift in the night.

As the pale dawn spread light through the room, Celia started to awake. For an instant, she was disoriented and surprised to find him tangled around her, but remembering the night, she smiled. Shifting gently away, she propped herself up to watch him while he slept.

Even after looking at him hundreds of times, his pure male beauty stung her anew. He was sprawled in the deepest of sleeps, as he had been the first morning of the flood. He'd tossed the sheets away in the heat, and so lay perfectly bare and open for her gaze.

She swallowed. His hair sprayed black across the white cotton pillowcase, curling around his strong neck and touching his broad shoulders. His mouth, soft and full in repose, looked tender amid the shadow of his unshaved beard. Lashes as long as a child's arched over the high plane of his cheekbones.

It was still hard to believe he was flesh and blood.

A gentle arousal weighed in her belly as she let her gaze travel over the sinewy arms and sleek chest, over the flat, hard belly and the big hands. A ripple seared through her as she looked at the oddly vulnerable weight of his sex, resting on his thigh—last night she had been just a bit alarmed to see the size of him. Her gaze moved lower, to the furred calves and the strong, bare feet with their high arches. Like his hands, his feet were beautiful, sculpted with graceful curves and lean lines.

She remembered the last morning they had awakened together in this room. The pale light was much the same then as now, and Celia remembered her wish that morning to straddle this rough and tender stranger.

Since then, she had learned so much more—learned of his lonely, lonely heart, his lost dreams and sad childhood and wandering life. She had learned her stranger could tease and fish; that he loved the blues and his sister and a wild, willful river named Jezebel.

Her heart caught in her throat. She loved him. Against her better judgment, against everything she'd dreamed she'd have, she loved him.

And this morning, her beautiful, restless drifter was lying still and quiet next to her. It might be her only chance.

Gently, she bent over him, teasingly running her hands over the plane of his belly and the rise of his ribs, watching in delight and terror as his eyelids flickered and another portion of his anatomy stirred to life. She moved closer, letting her breasts brush his body as she trailed kisses over his neck. He moved an arm sleepily to circle her shoulders.

Smiling at her own bravado, she touched the male heat of him, and the same iridescent bubble of pleasure that had made her laugh last night rose again within her at his response.

He awakened with a growl. "Celia! What are you doing?"

"Shh." She grinned at him mischievously, feeling her heart catch at the glowing sapphire of his eyes. Like the wanton woman in her vision, she threw her leg over him, tossing her hair over her shoulder to look down at him with a smile. He made a low, dark noise and reached for her.

But as they began to move again in the silent morning, her teasing slipped away, leaving behind the shining truth.

Eric called her name in a helpless voice, his hands bruising her shoulders, his lips in her hair. He clutched her to him with unwilling and almost desperate need.

He didn't know love any more than he knew happiness. As his breath, moist and warm, brushed her cheek and his scarred fingers held her, Celia knew she would lose him.

In spite of that, in spite of the foolishness of it, she whispered in his ear. "I love you, Eric."

It was a small thing, that single, heartfelt whisper, but at least he could take it with him when he left her. He enveloped her then, holding her so tightly she could scarcely breathe—as if he could keep her from slipping away.

They slept again. When Celia awakened, it was to find the bed empty. Alarmed, she sat up. He wouldn't leave without saying goodbye, would he?

"Celia." The word was heavy and deep.

She turned to see him crouched by the window, wearing his jeans and nothing else. On his neck were small marks made by her mouth, and his hair had not yet been combed; it tumbled in a glossy disarray around his face. "I thought you'd gone," she said.

"I wouldn't leave while you were sleeping," he said, and stood up. "But I need to get out and make some more phone calls about Laura."

His walls had slammed into place again—as if nothing had passed between them, as if he would just walk away and forget the night. Gathering the sheet around her, Celia sat up straight. "I thought," she said, testing, "that I might talk you into staying for that breakfast I never fixed you."

He closed his eyes. She watched his jaw clench one time, then he looked at her and she saw the loneliness screaming from the blue depths. He crossed the room and knelt by the bed, taking her hand. "Celia, I shouldn't have come here last night."

She yanked her hand from his grip. "Save it," she said harshly. "I can do without graceful parting words."

"Celia—"

"I mean it," she said, and stood up, taking the sheet with her. "I've had lots of practice with people who care for me only when it's convenient."

He reached for her again. "No, Celia—"

With a bitter smile, she dodged his touch. Shaking her head over her own illusions, she said, "I knew when I met you that it would be like this. I kept telling myself to leave it alone. To stay clear of you." She swallowed hard, clinging to her anger and frustration to keep the sorrow at bay.

"I'm sorry." His voice was subdued. "It was selfish of me to come here. I just wanted to see you."

Bright, life-giving anger surged through her. She lifted her chin. "Don't do it, Eric—don't cast yourself as one of Jacob Moon's tragic heroes, and don't you dare make me one of his weak, victim heroines."

"It's not like that!" he said. His eyes narrowed, his chin jutted forward and Celia knew he was going. "You're the one that keeps thinkin' I'm somebody I'm not." He grabbed a sock from the floor and stormed toward the door. On the threshold, he paused and looked back at her as if he would say something else. Then with a single shake of his head, he left her.

Only then did she allow herself to sink down onto the bed, her control crumbling. The scent of him clung to the pillow he had slept on, and Celia buried her face in it.

She was an idiot. A fool. A victim of her own fantasies. Eric wasn't the good and honest man she'd tried to believe he was. Or perhaps there was some goodness and honesty there, but it had long been buried by his restlessness and wandering.

She wept. Wept for him and for herself, for the perfect sweetness of their union and for all the days they would never share. Wept for her stupidity and romantic delusions, wept for the times she would miss him.

Then, because she was practical above all things, she dried her eyes and got up. They could no doubt use an extra pair of hands at the Red Cross station. And really, in light of the sorrows some of those people faced, a broken heart seemed a manageable affliction.

It was something of a mistake to go to the high school, Celia found. She busied herself in helping to prepare the noon meal for a slowly dwindling crowd, then bustled about performing various small tasks. A week and a half had passed since Jezebel had retreated, however, and the greatest portion of disasters the people had faced were now dealt with. A federal work crew had been dispatched to rebuild and repair the damage wrought by the water; relatives and friends

had taken in most of the homeless temporarily shel-
tered in the school gym, and even most of the missing
had been found. Except Laura. Laura was still missing.

Foiled in her attempt to stay busy, Celia went to her
classroom in the late afternoon. It was located on the
third floor of the old building, and the proportions
were satisfyingly grand. A bank of broad windows
faced south and showed a wide expanse of verdant
treetops punctuated with the rooftops of Gideon. Below, in a baseball field, a gaggle of youths pitched and
batted, caught fly balls and ran bases.

It was an extraordinarily peaceful scene. A painting of small-town America, just as she'd pictured it for
so many years.

What would it have been like to grow up here? She
rested a hip against the windowsill and frowned. What
would it have been like to attend this high school with
people she had known since kindergarten? Would she,
like Eric, want to leave this town by now?

She had missed the comfort of long-term friendships and the steadiness of familiar faces in her wandering childhood. But what had she gained?

She had gained Paris in the morning, had heard the
music of Italian voices in Milan. She had ridden a train
through the Alps and stared in awe at the stupendous
beauty of those history-drenched mountains. She had
sat in a German pub listening to the wild music of
Gypsies while her parents danced and drank dark beer.
She had watched her gloriously beautiful mother
dance *Sleeping Beauty* in ornate, centuries-old the-
aters and listened to her father read aloud in his boom-

ing, powerful voice words that he had written and words he had not.

All that early roaming had left her ready to settle in this small, quaint place—but if she had spent her childhood here, her curious heart would have led her away, just like so many others.

Lynn spoke from the door of the quiet room. "Celia. Thank heaven—I've been looking everywhere for you."

Struck by an odd tone in her friend's voice, Celia turned with a frown. "What is it?"

"I just got a call from some rescue workers." Her expression was heavy. "They found a man's body in a rowboat several miles downriver—they think it's Jake."

"Laura Putman's ex-husband."

"Right."

"Why did you need to find me for that?" Unconsciously, Celia crossed her arms.

Lynn gave her a knowing smile. "Honey, I've been around the block a time or two. I saw Eric walking from your house this morning." With a lift of her eyebrows, she added, "I've also seen more than one case of whisker burn."

Celia guiltily touched the raw pink place on her chin and flushed. "I should have stayed home today."

"No one but me would put it together." Lynn shrugged. "Anyway, someone needs to tell him, and I thought you might be the best one."

"I don't think so," Celia returned, biting her lip. She dusted the windowsill distractedly with her fingertips. "We didn't exactly part on the friendliest terms."

Lynn settled at one of the desks. "Come sit down for a minute. Whoever it is in that boat isn't going anywhere."

Celia hesitated.

"We need to talk," Lynn insisted, and patted the chair.

"I'm not all that sure I *want* to talk."

"Yeah, I know. Just like you didn't want to the other night." Steadfastly, Lynn pointed to the chair.

Rolling her eyes in defeat, feeling like a recalcitrant child and unable to help herself, Celia sat. "Talk away."

Lynn took Celia's hand and leaned over, her dark eyes penetrating and sharp. "Mmm," she murmured to herself. "I figure you must have hooked up with him during the flood at some point, since I saw you three days before that and you were fine."

Celia looked away.

"Did he get stranded there?"

With a sigh of defeat, Celia looked at Lynn with a reluctant smile. "You won't rest until you get the whole story, will you?"

"Now you're getting the idea."

"So Texans aren't just know-it-alls, they're nosy, too, huh?"

Lynn squeezed her fingers. "You're in love with him."

Briefly, Celia closed her eyes. Sarcastically she said, "It was such wise decision on my part. I knew better—but I can't seem to help it."

"Love doesn't pay much attention to shoulds," Lynn said quietly. "I can't tell you your business—but he needs something, that's for sure."

"I have serious doubts that he'll find it in Gideon."

Lynn pursed her lips, then smiled. "His attitude has been pretty bad for a while now, I'll grant you that. But I have the advantage of having known him a long time, and I know from having seen what he was and where he came from that he's one of the original fighters." She paused, shaking her head. "That uncle of his drank up nearly every damned penny Eric earned—and he worked hard, you understand. Did everything—pumped gas and washed windows and mowed lawns."

Gently, he stroked Celia's hand. "Nobody really ever took him seriously, though—they all figured sooner or later he'd end up like the rest of his kin. You didn't grow up around here—you just can't know how it is to be white and poor." She smiled. "Anyway, then Willie Hormel taught him guitar." She snapped her fingers. "Eric got to where he walked proud, no matter what anybody said."

Celia frowned and opened her mouth to speak, but Lynn forestalled her with one uplifted palm.

"You want to know why he's got such a bad attitude and I'm getting to that."

In spite of herself, Celia felt a brief flicker of amusement. Her father, too, had told stories this way. How many times had she heard her mother sigh in exasperation, "For heaven's sake, Jacob, just get to the point!"?

"Well, you know that he left when he was about sixteen or so. It had to have been hard for him out there, but he made his mark. He was a big deal when he came home—those songs he wrote and the fact that he'd played with everybody who was anybody in the blues. The folks around here, well, most of them are happy just to have enough to pay the bills and buy a new used car every few years. Your daddy and Eric Putman went out there and got themselves famous."

Slowly, now, the point of Lynn's tale was emerging. Celia waited.

"A few years ago, when he came home for Laura's wedding, there was a girl who followed him wherever he went. She was a lot like him in some ways—she wanted to be somebody, and nobody had ever taken the time to tell her she *was*. She'd been one of my students, the first year I started teaching."

"Retta," Celia said.

"He told you about her?"

"A little. Just the accident."

"He blames himself for it," Lynn said with a shake of her head. "But there's people who just have a violent end written all over them, and Retta was one even back in high school. She drank too much and she gave herself away—" Lynn made a sad noise. "She and Eric were too much alike."

"What do you mean?"

Lynn bit her lip for a moment, and Celia could see she wasn't absolutely certain she ought to go on.

"Come on, Lynn," Celia said. "You've gone this far, you may as well go all the way."

Lynn nodded. "They neither one of them had any sense of who they were, because there'd never been anyone to tell them they were something besides beautiful. Eric found his guitar and something else to hang on to, but Retta never did. I kept thinking he'd be able to help her, but he didn't love her—not the way she wanted him to. He took her with him because he saw himself. I think, if Retta hadn't been so dead set on destroying herself, Eric would have probably married her, love or not. But that wasn't enough for Retta."

The thought of Eric married to someone else, someone he didn't love, pierced Celia. She bowed her head, knowing the next part of the story—but she wanted to hear it from Lynn, who'd already given a new slant to everything else.

"When he had the accident, he came home for a little while, just to mend. Retta's brothers called him a murderer, and there were some folks who were unkind about the life-style they thought musicians indulged in—you know?"

A conversation wafted through Celia's mind. *Do people still have babies christened? Around here, they sure do. This is the Bible Belt, sister.* "I can imagine," she said.

"So he lost his guitar, which was all he thought he had, and he came home to the same kind of ugliness he knew when he was a child." Lynn straightened. "But the worst thing was that he couldn't save Retta—which in his mind was pretty close to saying he couldn't save himself, either."

Celia rubbed her face. "Sometimes I feel like I'm lost in one of my father's books. Why do all these people believe all these things?"

"You haven't read enough if you have to ask."

In surprise, Celia looked up. "You've read his books?"

"Of course I have—he's our hometown hero!" More seriously, she added, "He was a great writer, Celia, but you have to look pretty deep to see what he was trying to say. I don't think he meant to be obtuse. He just couldn't look at Gideon head on."

Celia didn't want to talk about her father. The man was dead, and Lynn had sought her out and told her this story for a reason. "Why did you tell me all these things?"

"If something happens to Laura—" Lynn shook her head. "He's gonna need somebody in his corner, Celia. You are that somebody, whether or not either one of you knows it."

"Do you mother everyone in Gideon this way?"

Lynn smiled. "Pretty close. Will you go give him the message?"

Celia made a sound of annoyance. "Yes. I'll give it to him."

"In person."

"Yes."

Lynn hugged her. "Thank you." Without releasing her, Lynn lifted her head. "He really is a man worth knowing. Try to remember how hard things have been for him—don't give up."

"I'm not going to talk about this again. Do you understand?"

Lynn chuckled. "I read you loud and clear."

The suppertime odor of frying meat filled the air as Celia drove to Eric's house. Or rather, she corrected herself, his sister's house. He didn't have one.

She parked and climbed out of the car as calmly as she could. The front door was open and from within came the sound of voices, laughter, a quick squeal of guitar.

Bitterly Celia thought it hadn't taken Eric very long to recover from the night. But then, men were like that, weren't they? Able to engage their bodies without engaging their emotions. Too bad, she thought going up the swept path, women didn't operate in the same way.

No matter what Lynn said, Celia was still furiously angry with him. And she didn't care if it was irrational, if she had encouraged him, if it was wrong. Anger was safer than some of the other things she might feel if she let it go.

She knocked on the screen door, bracing herself to deliver her message. Eric appeared, for once wearing his shoes and a shirt—a turquoise T-shirt with New Orleans emblazoned over the front. The color lent his eyes a peculiar intensity.

He frowned, puzzled. "Hi, Celia. Come on in."

She nearly protested, but he'd pushed open the door and moved aside to give her passage, and there was nothing else to do. Bowing her head to avoid looking at him, she brushed past him.

A thin, dark youth sat on the couch, a guitar in his lap. He greeted her cheerfully. "Hi."

"Celia," Eric said, "this is James. He's a blues guitarist."

"Hello," she said, politely, and bit her lip. She didn't know if she ought to deliver her message in front of this earnest young man or not. But if she asked to speak to Eric privately, he might construe an entirely different meaning from the request. An untenable thought.

"I don't want to keep you," she said, her voice brusque. "Lynn asked me to tell you they've found Laura's ex-husband. Or they think they have—no one has identified the body positively yet."

Every scrap of color drained abruptly from Eric's face. He sank into an armchair. "He's dead?"

Celia nodded.

"Where? How'd they find him—I mean, was Laura—"

"He was in a rowboat," she said. "They didn't really know why or what he was doing." She took a breath. "There was no sign of Laura."

For an instant, he seemed to crumple. Not outwardly. He simply sat in his chair, his hands folded loosely between his knees. Outwardly, Eric looked as sturdy as a live oak, but Celia could see the contraction of muscles, the wince of terror, the bleakness of his horror. Even through her anger, she felt a pluck of sympathy.

She cleared her throat. "I'll drive you over there," she said quietly. "You can see for yourself."

James rose. "I'll come back another time."

Distractedly, Eric looked at the youth. "Sorry."

"That's all right, man. Family comes first. I understand that." With a smile, he dipped his head toward Celia. "It was nice to meet you."

"You, too," she said.

Even after James ambled out, Eric didn't move. He just sat there, staring sightlessly at the floor. Celia hesitated, looking around her at the collections of the missing Laura. It was a warm room, with begonias blooming in the windows and a tidy arrangement of books along one wall. The color scheme was a little odd for Celia's taste, with splashes of red and purple and green against walls of cream. Gold-threaded pillows in the same mix of wild color decorated the couch.

"She must be something else," Celia commented, smiling. "A little crazy, but sweet."

Eric didn't reply. His stillness broke suddenly as he took a long hard breath and bent his head into his hand, pressing a fist against a spot on his forehead. "Lord have mercy," he whispered roughly, and it was plain the words were as close as he could get to a prayer.

Gently, Celia touched his arm. "Come with me, Eric. You'll feel better once you see she's not there."

"Will I, Celia?"

His midnight eyes glowed with the hollowness of an empty mine shaft. She thought of Lynn's warning: if his sister died, he'd have nothing left.

"Let's go," she said firmly.

Chapter Eleven

The drive was utterly silent. Eric hunched next to her in the seat of her economy car like a caged animal, and Celia thought fleetingly that he and her father were both as big as grizzly bears. It was too bad the pair of them had never met. They would have been quite comfortable together.

"Pull off on that little turn there," he said as they approached a bridge. It was a bigger bridge than many of the others spanning Jezebel's dozens of creeks and tributaries that ribboned through the landscape. This bridge spanned the river herself at a spot where she ran fast and clear over a tumble of boulders. A rescue van was parked on the shoulder of the road. Celia pulled up behind it.

A cluster of women sobbed as a sheet-draped body was reeled up the embankment. The lights of the rescue van flashed monotonously and as they climbed out of the car, she could hear the muted, intermittent growl of a police scanner.

A fist of memory slugged her body. She flashed on herself standing on the side of a cliff in Italy, seeing below the ruined remains of her father's car, heard the singing, sympathetic voice of the young man who had been nominated to tell her that her father was dead.

She blinked hard, forcing herself back to the moment by focusing on the trio of weeping women at the side of the road. There was an older woman with cat-eye glasses and a sleeveless cotton shirt over green and pink polyester pants. A double row of pin curls looped around her head.

The two girls, teenagers, were obviously her daughters. They huddled close to their mother, peering toward the river with reddened eyes.

Eric brushed past Celia toward the embankment, his dark face closed tight. As he passed the trio of women, the mother cried out and tore herself from the grasp of her daughters to lunge at him, uttering an almost unearthly sound of rage, deep and guttural. Her straight-armed thrust caught Eric on the shoulder and knocked him sideways. He stumbled under the force, and startled, not quite understanding that he'd been attacked, he reached for the woman as if to steady her.

Celia watched in horror as the woman found her footing and slugged him. Eric staggered and lifted one arm to ward off another blow. The woman, making shrill, animalistic noises, pushed him again and they tumbled down the steep slope, locked in an angry embrace.

The woman flung her fists wildly, pummeling Eric wherever she could reach him. Most blows glanced off his shoulders and arms and chest, but one landed square in his mouth.

"Mama!" the girls cried in unison, and ran after her. "Mama, stop it!"

By the time Celia found the presence of mind to follow, Eric had gained his footing and held the woman in a hard grip against his chest. One of his hands wrapped around both the woman's wrists as he blotted the blood away from his lip.

He looked utterly disinterested in spite of the obscenities the woman screamed into the evening air: slurs upon Eric, his mother, his sister. The girls grabbed her.

"Get her out of my sight before I kill her," Eric said in a harsh, low voice.

And still the woman screamed obscenities. Celia paused in front of her as the girls dragged her up the hill. The girls both looked at her with alarm. Celia narrowed her eyes, her fists clenched at her side. "Why don't you hit someone who can hit you back?"

The younger of the two girls, her eyes welling with tears, whispered, "She's just crazy with grief. She don't mean it."

Celia shook her head and moved aside. She joined Eric, who stood next to a battered row boat, talking with the ambulance driver. As she approached, the man clapped Eric on the shoulder and, with a nod to Celia, headed back up the hill.

"He said there was no sign of anybody else being in the boat with Jake when it got caught under the pilings," Eric said quietly. "They've been through the woods all around and didn't find any footprints or anything like that."

Celia nodded. Anything she said would be hollow under the circumstances.

He bent over the boat suddenly and grabbed a muddy bit of cloth. As he tugged it out, Celia saw that it was a scarf, red and purple and gold, with a fringe. She felt a catch in her throat.

Eric turned to her, holding up the scarf. His lip was bleeding. A leaf clung to his hair from his tumble down the embankment. And in his eyes was such hopeless grief that all of Celia's hurt pride and anger instantly dissolved. She stepped forward without a word and hugged him.

He clung to her with desperation and terror, making no sound. Celia felt his need as if he were a light-starved plant, crawling through crevices and cracks to find the sun.

Which man was he? The broken bluesman with no future, or the troubled, lonely man who needed to set down roots before he died? She wished she could decide.

Eric tried, on the way back to Laura's house, to find words to thank Celia for the comfort she offered so easily. He struggled with ways to tell her how much he needed her calm, her simple and uncomplicated offerings, how much it meant.

But he kept coming back to the fact that he'd stepped over the line last night. There was no way to make that right, not with a woman like Celia.

So he didn't speak until she pulled up in front of the house. If he asked, she would come inside with him, would sit with him as long as necessary. This morning he'd managed to kill the light of hero worship in her eyes, but now there was something deeper. Compassion, maybe.

For a moment he sat in the cramped seat of her car, listening to the small engine idle. A part of him ached to reach for her, to bury his face in her hair and— what? Take more from her? He'd already taken enough.

He clenched his fist against the urge because he knew he'd have to leave her behind eventually. He'd been wrong last night to go to her, more wrong than he'd ever been about anything. Somehow, he had to undo the damage.

"I appreciate your coming with me," he said finally. "I guess tomorrow I'll start calling around again."

She touched his hand. "Why don't you come with me and let me fix you some supper?"

"No, Celia."

She snatched her hand away as if she had been burned. A stab of something sad cut through his belly. Once again, he was handling everything wrong. "I didn't mean it like that, sugar," he said.

"Don't call me that." She stared straight ahead, her hands crossed over the steering wheel.

He stared at her, surprised, then remembered his own words last night. *You're so beautiful, Celia. Like sugar.* And she was. She made him feel as though he'd gotten lost in some fairy-tale land of happy endings, lost in the scene of spun sugar on top of a cake.

As he stared at her silvery hair and the smooth, delicate profile, he found himself lifting his hand—a gesture he caught and stopped halfway. "I didn't mean to hurt your feelings," he said. "Not now, not ever."

She looked down, hiding her face behind her hair. This time, he couldn't stop himself. He reached over to brush her hair gently away from the rose-tinted cheek. "I mean it, Celia. I tried hard to keep away from you. But you really are as sweet as sugar, as sweet as morning, and I couldn't."

Her lips set in a hard line.

Undeterred, Eric tucked the silky locks behind her ear and traced the lobe lightly. "You still really think you can reform me, Celia."

She looked at him. "That's ridiculous."

He lifted his eyebrows. "Maybe *reform* is a bad word, then. Try heal. Or enlighten." Her dark lashes swept downward once more and he knew he was right. "I'm not worth the time you'd spend, Celia."

"That's where you're wrong, Eric," she began earnestly.

"Shh. I don't mean that I'm no good. Just that I'm not the kind of man you need. You need somebody stable, somebody willing to put down roots and raise those babies you want." He swallowed. "No matter how hard I tried, I'd never be able to be that man."

Any other woman he'd ever met would have looked at him then with tears glimmering in the corners of her eyes. But Celia, as usual, surprised him.

With a long-suffering sigh, she rolled her eyes. "It would make a great song," she said. "Now, would you please get out of my car and let me go get something to eat?"

Thrown off center, Eric frowned and opened the door. "Sure. Thanks again," he said.

"Anytime." Then she drove off, leaving him to stand alone in the darkness, his belly growling with hunger, his chest aching with loss and confusion and something he couldn't name.

He bit back a grin. That was a lie. That third emotion was pure admiration. She was really something.

Shaking his head at both of them, he went inside to fix himself something to eat. Provisions were getting low and he had to make do with fried eggs and bacon. As he settled the ingredients on the table, a grip of restlessness caught him and he reached for the flour and baking powder, as well. A half-empty carton of buttermilk had been tickling his appetite for several days, and he smelled it to make sure it was still good.

Laura always made biscuits for breakfast the first morning when he visited. As he stirred the dry ingredients together with a fork, he smiled again, thinking he'd been waiting to eat biscuits until she could make them for him. Trouble was, she wasn't much of a cook. Never had been. He ate the tough, crispy biscuits she cooked because he loved her.

This time, he'd have the real thing.

There was a small cassette player on the counter and he flipped it on, pressing the button to play a favorite tape he carried with him—a hodgepodge of blues favorites, as eclectic as it was good. New and old, guitar and harmonica, country blues and Delta blues and city blues. Even a little Roberta Flack for a soulful touch.

The music filled the room with a comforting sound, and he put bacon in a pan to fry. With a deft touch, he mixed buttermilk into the flour for his biscuits, stirred just long enough to moisten the dough, then rolled and cut it with an economy of motion learned in a hundred little cafés on the road before his luck had turned.

He slipped the pan of biscuits into the oven, humming along with the music. Cooking had been one of the only little jobs he could stand. His mechanical skills were nil, and although he could do carpentry and concrete work as well as anyone, he hated the long hours and hot work. At least in a kitchen, there were waitresses to flirt with and music to listen to.

As he stirred the eggs, he pursed his lips. A little café, now that might be work he wouldn't mind, something to fill the void left by workless hands that had spent a lifetime at some kind of industry. The past two years, he hadn't worked because he didn't need the money—his long habit of frugality and careful husbandry had also seen to that. Canny investments had turned his song royalties and concert gigs and road trips into a nest egg big enough so he wouldn't *have* to work the rest of his life if he was careful. Royalties from his songs and records would continue to come.

And in spite of everything, he doubted he'd quit writing songs, even if he couldn't play them.

But he found he wanted to work. It was unnatural for a man to spend his days idle.

He reached for a plate from the shelf as his eggs cooked, then frowned at the black ceramic-ware. His sister was just plain weird in some ways, he thought as he put it back and dug at the bottom of the stack for plain white china. Much better. He dished out the eggs, drained the bacon and bent to remove the biscuits.

Perfect. Fluffy and lightly browned. He ate five with apple jelly—probably made from juice if he knew short-cut Laura—and generous helpings of butter.

It was only as he cleared the meal and looked out to the black night that he let the situation filter back into his mind.

It was dark; dark and hot and filled with bugs. Was Laura out there somewhere, alone and afraid? Her fear of snakes made Celia's look like friendliness, and she hated creepy-crawlies with a passion. She didn't like to rough it or to get dirty. To think his sister was out there in those dark woods alone made him feel sick.

He wandered into the living room and picked up the scarf he'd found in the boat. It had shattered him upon finding it—a kind of shock had first set in when Celia had announced they'd found Jake's body. It hadn't really dissipated until he'd put a solid meal in his belly.

Chewing his lip, he pulled the silky fabric through his fingers, back and forth between his left and right hands. At some point, Laura had been in that boat—a damned rowboat—while Jezebel was flooding.

Jake had been in Gideon all his life, too. He would have known it was suicidal to take that tiny boat out on the river. And it had proved to be so.

A scenario began to piece itself together in Eric's mind as the fabric swished through his fingers, back and forth, back and forth. Jake had always been crazy. He'd fought in high school, fought in bars when he drank too much, was prone to wild drives down dark country roads in his truck.

But none of it seemed dangerous in the old days. Restless country boys fought and drove fast to relieve their boredom.

Jake and Laura had dated off and on all through high school, but had broken up when Laura went to Dallas for her training. She had lived there a few years, then returned to Gideon. She and Jake had just naturally drifted together, got married.

It hadn't seemed any worse than any other match she might have made. Eric had come home for the wedding, but because of Retta, he hadn't come home again for a long time after.

Following his accident, Eric realized Jake was more than a wild redneck. He was crazy. He was so jealous Laura couldn't even go to the grocery store alone, so jealous he was furious over Eric's return.

Laura begged him to get counseling and had gone for some herself. Jake would have none of it.

A year ago he'd beaten Laura for making a phone call he didn't approve. She had landed in the hospital with a broken arm and a dislocated shoulder. She'd filed for divorce the next day.

But Jake wouldn't leave it alone. Eric had been on his way to stay with Laura until the bastard got the message when the flood stranded him at Celia's.

Had Jake known Eric was coming? Maybe he had seen the flood as his last chance. He'd kidnapped Laura and set them both afloat on the rising river, knowing they would drown.

A chill touched his chest. It made sense with the sick reasoning Jake would have used. There was also the fact that Jake's mother had blamed Eric for Jake's death, which meant she knew more than she let on.

Could Laura possibly have survived the flood in a rowboat? Could she have been thrown overboard and managed to swim to safety? Or had she drowned and been swept so far downriver, no one had found her yet?

He shoved that grim scenario away. Laura had survived one flood. He had to believe she had the resources to survive another.

He picked up his guitar case and flipped it open. He lifted the instrument and held it, stroking the sleek, cool lines, taking pleasure in the shielded feeling it gave him.

He bent his head again to tune the strings. But before he could pluck a single note, the strident, shattering sound of the phone cut into the quiet room.

Dread slammed his body. Another ring screamed out. He stared at the red instrument with horror. It rang again.

Slowly, he got to his feet.

*   *   *

Rather than go home, Celia went back to the school. Lynn had gone home, as had most of the other volunteers. A game of basketball was going on between a group of teenage boys in the gymnasium, and the hollow, slapping sound of their ball echoed in the empty halls. Faintly, below the sound of their play, came the slight clink of dishes being washed in the kitchen.

Celia headed for the auditorium, gathered up the computer lists and marched to the office and the phones. She had to end this once and for all. Once Eric found out what happened to Laura, he'd move on. The sooner the better. If Laura didn't surface soon, Eric Putman was going to leave the shards of Celia's heart in a trail from Gideon to the ends of the earth.

Armed with the lists and phone books from every county in Jezebel's path, she sat down and started dialing. She called sheriff's offices, ambulance companies, hospitals, Red Cross centers—every possible source of information.

It took hours. Each source had to double-check lists and descriptions and anything new they'd found. One woman at a sheriff's office in a nearby county heard the description Celia gave and said, "That sounds like a woman we found this afternoon. Hang on."

Heart in her throat, Celia held the line. A small headache had begun to pound in her temples, and her neck ached with fatigue. It had been an awfully long night and day, after all. Her body screamed for rest and food.

"Hello?" the woman said.

"I'm here."

"We have a body fitting the description you gave. Do you have a name?"

No! Celia's mind screamed as she remembered the way Eric had crumpled this afternoon. "Laura Putman," she said, her voice tight.

"Okay. You'll have to keep lookin', honey. This is a different woman. Her identification was found on her."

"Thank you." Celia hung up and collapsed on the desk, her head on her arms. She trembled violently, giving in to her terror for a moment. A thread of sorrow wound around her heart for the family and friends of the other woman, and once again she counted her blessings that she and everyone she cared about had come through the flood safely.

Part of her trembling was hunger, she realized dimly, and she promised her empty stomach she'd fill it as soon as she finished the calls. There were only two more names on the list.

Both fruitless, it turned out. Defeated, Celia stood up and started to round the desk to go beg food from the kitchen. She nearly tripped on a slim, tiny phone book for a town she'd never heard of.

She put it on the desk, rubbing the back of her neck. In the kitchen, she coaxed the cook out of a roll and a cold slice of roast beef to tide her over until she could get home. But on a hunch, she paused on her way out of the kitchen. "Have you ever heard of a town called Calla's Folly?"

"Sure, I've heard of it. Get's wiped out every spring by the flood. That's why they call it that. The river's bound and determined the town's gonna belong to her before too much longer.''

"I thought it was the Mississippi that did that kind of thing.''

"Nah. Most any river with any spirit takes a town every so often.''

Celia smiled and nodded, then pulled her keys from her purse. A hot shower and a good night's sleep sounded heavenly.

But at the doors, she paused. What could it hurt to make just one or two more calls?

The Sheriff's Department in Calla's Folly referred her to a clinic that wasn't even listed in the phone book. There, a pleasantly energetic woman answered the phone, and when Celia asked again about a woman fitting Laura's description, she said, "You're in luck tonight.''

"I am?''

"Mmm-hmm. We found a woman like that this very morning. She's unconscious and critically dehydrated, but I reckon she'll live.''

"Has she awakened?''

"Not yet. Might be tomorrow morning.''

"No identification?''

"No, I'm sorry. You'll have to come see her yourself, I'm afraid. Sure does sound like the woman you described.''

"I'll be there,'' Celia said. "I have to drive from Gideon, so it'll be an hour or so.''

As she hung up the phone, she thought of fetching Eric to drive along with her. Then she remembered the false alarm of a few minutes before and decided he'd had about as much as he could take. If she had to sit by the woman's bed all night until she awakened, at least Eric would be spared more worry. If the woman turned out to be Laura, nothing would be lost—Celia would just call to let him know.

If it wasn't Laura, well, at least he would be spared another false hope.

Chapter Twelve

By the time she reached Calla's Folly, Celia was truly exhausted. Her neck ached, her head pounded, her eyes were grainy. Muscles she didn't even know existed ached from the vigorous night she'd spent with Eric.

Outside the friendly, brightly lit clinic, she paused. Jezebel had come through here screaming. A tree branch clung to the roof of a house across the road, sticking comically into the starry sky like an antler.

The clinic had obviously received first priority in the cleanup effort, however, for as Celia walked in, she saw that the floors were waxed, the lights bright. The walls could have used a fresh coat of paint, but that was, after all, a minor point.

A stout woman behind the desk looked up as Celia approached. "Hello. Are you the one who called about the woman we found?"

"Yes."

The nurse waddled around the counter. "Come with me."

Celia followed her down a hallway, hearing the squeak of rubber-soled shoes against clean linoleum. The nurse pushed open a big door and stepped aside for Celia to pass.

Inside the room, Celia paused. There, covered with a crisp sheet, was Laura. There was no question that it was Eric's sister lying so still in the bed. Her hair was long, trailing over a shapely figure, and it was every bit as black and wavy as her brother's. There was the same mouth, fuller and riper in this woman's face, but unmistakable. Even the sweep of lashes over the high cheekbones was the same.

Like Eric, Laura was uncommonly, compellingly beautiful, even with a pallor and bruises marring her face.

Celia nodded at the nurse, who winked and left her. She crossed the room to take one of the still woman's hands. "Laura," she said softly, "can you hear me?"

There was no response.

Celia stroked the slender hand. "Your brother is going to be so happy to see you. He's been crazy with worry."

There was a tiny flicker of eyelids in the still face and a jerky movement of a thumb against Celia's palm.

Suddenly Laura was looking right at her, with eyes a stunning, rich shade of blue. Celia smiled and squeezed her hand. "Your mother must have been quite a beauty," she said, not caring if it made sense.

Laura licked her lips and her eyelids drifted to half mast. "Mama was blond," she whispered. "Like you."

Even in the weakness of the words, Celia heard the husky beauty of Laura's voice. Patting her hand, she said, "I'm going to go call your brother. I'll be right back."

In the hallway she found a pay phone and realized she had to look up the telephone number. It seemed odd after all they had shared, but until now, there had been no reason to call him.

The phone rang five times before he picked it up, and Celia winced at the wary, harsh sound of his voice.

"Eric, I found Laura. She's alive."

"What?"

"She's alive. She's in a clinic in Calla's Folly."

"How do you know it's her?"

"I'm here with her now, Eric. There's no question that she's your sister. The two of you could be twins."

"Calla's Folly?" he asked.

"A little clinic here. You can't miss it."

"I'll be right there. Will you stay with her until I can get there?"

"I don't think so," Celia protested. She didn't want to see him. It would just make it harder. "I'm very tired."

A pause traveled over the wire. "All right, then. I understand."

Guilt washed through her. It was a small thing to ask, after all. He didn't want Laura to be alone. "I'll stay."

"No, that's okay. I'm sure she's in good hands. You've done so much already—thank you, Celia."

"I'll stay. Get in your car and get here. I'm exhausted."

"Then go on home," he said firmly. "I mean it."

She was suddenly too tired to argue or care anymore. "All right. Goodbye, Eric."

She hung up before he could reply, a deep plucking sensation in her chest.

Laura.

At the door of the hospital room, Eric paused, his knees shivery with relief. Celia sat alongside his sister in a chair and she jumped up.

"I didn't stay for your sake," she said defensively, folding a newspaper and putting it down on the chair.

"I don't care why you stayed." He crossed the short space to the bed and took Laura's hand gently, drinking in the precious, achingly familiar sight of her beloved face. For long, long moments, all he could do was stare at her, his Laura. Alive. He smoothed a tangled mass of hair from her neck and gently kissed her cheek.

Then he let go of a long-held breath and rested his forehead briefly against her temple, taking joy in the warmth of her flesh. "Thank God," he whispered.

Finally he looked at Celia. "And thank you." He swallowed, wishing he could cross the empty space between them. He needed to hold her close to him, to have her somehow absorb the excess of gratitude and relief he felt pouring from him like sweat.

He couldn't seem to take that first step, however, and instead, he just looked at her, hoping she could see what he couldn't say. His thanks meant so many things—that she'd found Laura, that she'd stayed, that she *cared*.

She stood silently, absorbing his messages with her great, pale ice eyes.

"I don't know how I can ever repay you," he said.

And now in the ethereal face there glowed a hunger, a pain, a plucking wish—all of which he'd planted. She dropped her gaze and set her stubborn mouth in a strong line. "I was glad to help." Her laugh was soft and self-mocking. "It makes me feel like a good neighbor."

He nodded.

She gathered her purse. "I'll leave you two alone now." She passed him and paused to look once more at the sleeping Laura. "I really was glad to help," she said, and patted his arm, squeezing a little around the elbow like a friendly matron.

He recognized a defense when he saw one and didn't breach it as he'd breached so many others. For once he left well enough alone—let her go and didn't say a word to hold her back.

"Eric, will you stop waiting on me?" Laura exclaimed in some irritation from her perch on the couch.

"You don't need to be up running around just yet. Doc said it would take a few days to get your strength back."

"I've been home *five,* brother dear." She rolled her eyes. "Get over here and sit down. I want to talk to you."

Warily, Eric sunk into the chair adjacent to the couch. He had to admit she looked better: her bruises were faded to a pale yellow, and her robust good health had reasserted itself in the clear whites of her eyes and the ruddy color in her cheeks. "I get the message," he said. "You're okay."

"I'm better than okay." She touched his nose. "I'm free—God forgive me for being happy about anybody dyin', but I don't have to worry about Jake anymore." She smiled gently. "It's you I'm a little worried about."

He frowned.

"Oh, don't give me that look. You can bluff the rest of the world into thinkin' you're a big, tough guy, but I know you better than that."

Eric felt a little panic building in his chest, a purely defensive need to hide—even from his sister—the connection he'd discovered with Celia. For five days he'd managed to keep his thoughts on hold. If his sister started poking around in his heart, he'd be truly lost.

But her words surprised him. "The flood really upset you, didn't it?"

"Well, I—"

But typically, Laura pressed on. "You seem so vulnerable, and I know the last couple of years have been real hard on you, but it goes deeper than that. I've been thinking about it, and all I can come up with is that the flood brought up a lot of old memories for you."

"Laura, it's not the flood. It's Gideon." He jumped up and walked to the window, restless. "The flood just made me remember how much I hate this place, how much I hate all of this." Unconsciously, he clenched his fist at his side. "Then you were missing for so long, and I guess it was the last straw."

Soundlessly she crept up behind him and hugged him. "When are you going to stop running, Eric Putman?"

"Running?" He turned, uncomfortably reminded of the afternoon at the river when Celia had confronted him. "I just don't want to be *here.*"

She crossed her arms and lifted her eyebrows, her mouth taking a skeptical line. "That's the biggest lie of all." She shook her head. "I just wish I knew what you were looking for. Maybe then I could help you find it, help you finally be happy. You deserve it, little brother."

Something inside of him recoiled. "Like hell," he growled, and spun on his heel, heading for the door.

Her voice, rich and laced with amusement, stopped him. "You don't have to run from me, Eric. I love you no matter what."

He closed his eyes. "That's not fair."

"Life's like that." She took his hand. "Why don't you let me cook up something good for supper? I'll even make biscuits, since we missed your coming-home breakfast."

He licked a threatening smile from his lips and relented. He didn't have to act like an ass with Laura. It wouldn't matter anyway. Nothing he did would drive her away. Thinking of her crispy biscuits, however, made it hard for him to keep a straight face. "Sounds great."

"Good." She nodded to herself and bent to straighten a stack of magazines on the coffee table. Then, as if just remembering something puzzling, she said, "Eric?"

His eyebrows rose. "Laura?"

"Was there a woman in my hospital room before you got there?" She peered sightlessly at the wall, reaching for the elusive memory. "Small, all kind of silvery—" She broke off and looked at him. "Am I crazy?"

"No." He cleared his throat. "Her name's Celia Moon. She'd tracked you down and sat with you until I could get there."

Laura let go of a peal of laughter. "Whew," she said, touching her chest. "I thought she was an angel that night, you know. I've been afraid to ask in case she wasn't really there."

Eric remained silent, afraid anything he said would give him away.

Laura didn't seem to notice. She folded an afghan. "Moon. Is she kin to that writer?"

"His daughter. She's living in their old farmhouse."

"I wonder why I haven't met her yet?"

Restlessly, Eric moved, looking for something to do. "I don't think she'd been here that long. A few months, maybe."

Laura's gaze sharpened and he ducked it and squatted over the body of his guitar. "How do you know her?"

For an instant he almost lied. But she'd hear the story from someone else, and then he'd be even more cornered. He touched his nose. "I, uh, got stranded at her house during the flood."

"I thought you were here!"

He shook his head. "My car got stuck in that little creek by the Tyler's farm. I set out on foot, but it just got bad—I nearly drowned trying to ford another creek, and I knew I wouldn't be able to cross the river." He shrugged. "When I saw the lights at the Moons' house, I went there. She took me in."

"I see." A hard note sounded in Laura's words, and Eric looked up to see her standing in the middle of the room with her hands on her hips. "What kind of neighbor are you, anyway? She took you in and gave you shelter in the storm, then found me for you, and you haven't even called her to say thank you!" She made a little noise of disgust. "I can't believe your manners."

"I thanked her."

"Well," Laura said, "I'm going to thank her *properly.*" She moved toward the phone.

"Laura," Eric said in protest.

But she'd already set her mind on her course. The phone was in her hand.

* * *

Celia had tried every possible polite excuse she could think of to get out of going to dinner at Laura's house, but Laura was gently, politely insistent. In the end, she won out.

So in spite of her sweaty palms and aching heart, in spite of her resolve to stay clear of Eric until she could overcome her feelings for him, here Celia was, walking up the path once again. And once again, there he sat, on the porch, harmonica in hand. The notes he played danced with the sound of crickets in the brush and the dying calls of birds twittering in the branches of the trees. On the step sat a cat, its eyes sleepy, its ears alert as if it was listening.

Celia braced herself this time. All the way over, she'd reminded herself of Eric's physical details, calling up the most stunning of them in particular, so they wouldn't be such a shock.

It didn't help. He was like a sunset; she could remember the beauty and the sense of awe she felt, could summon the words for the details that so enchanted her, but each time she saw him was a brand-new experience, more compelling than her mind could hold for memory's sake.

The sight of his big, dark head, bent over the mournful notes of his harp, sent a wave of desire washing through her belly. Then he caught sight of her and stood up, broad and graceful and strong, and simply looked at her. He was polished, as if for special company, and Celia allowed herself a small smile, for she knew that was Laura's doing. His hair was carefully brushed, his shirt pressed, his feet shod in boots.

"Hello, Celia," he said.

She wanted to close her eyes against the sound of that dark, raw voice, but forced herself to stand there as if he didn't bother her, as if she were composed.

For another minute, they simply stood there, Eric on the porch, Celia in the yard, the cat between them. A breeze lifted a lock of his hair. It was impossible to read anything in his expression—his walls were firmly, rigidly in place.

Laura appeared at the screen door, a flutter of red silk and gold fringe. "Why, Eric Putman, your manners are in the sewer." She banged out the door and brushed past her brother. "I apologize, Celia—you are Celia?—he's been among men for too long."

Celia glanced at Eric. He smiled, as if sharing a secret with her. Infinitesimally, he shook his head.

Celia looked at Laura. "It's all right."

"Come on in," Laura urged, taking Celia's arm. "I'm just about to set the table. You and I can get acquainted while I'm doing it."

Overwhelmed, Celia let herself be led up the stairs, past Eric—who still grinned, as if in relief—and into the house.

Whatever she'd been expecting, this night was not it, Celia thought later as Laura served fat slices of chocolate cake. Eric sat directly across from her, speaking little, avoiding her gaze except for the occasional glimmer of humor she caught over one thing or another Laura did.

Laura herself was quite a surprise. The song Eric had sung on Celia's porch of the delicate, vulnerable woman looking for a home and gentle arms to hold her had nothing to do with the talkative whirlwind who served burned biscuits and cherry Kool-Aid with a supper otherwise wonderfully well cooked. She flitted around the room like a scarlet bird, her long, black hair flying, her jewelry glittering. Dazzling.

"So, tell me, Celia," Laura said as they ate the sinfully rich cake. "You plan to stay in Gideon?"

"Definitely," Celia replied. "I spent most of my life trying to get here."

"That's nice. I hope we'll be friends." With a droll glance toward her brother, Laura added, "I love Gideon, except when it comes to shopping. I go into Dallas for the big things. Have you been there?"

"No," Celia admitted. "I'm a little afraid of the freeways."

"Oh, it's not so bad once you get used to it. Next time I go, I'll call you. I know all the best little spots to find bargains."

Celia glanced toward Eric, who silently ate his cake, outwardly calm. But she could sense the restlessness that brewed just below the surface and wondered what was bothering him. "Do you like Dallas, Eric?" she asked.

He lifted his shoulder in a single shrug. "I guess."

"Do you like anything tonight, Eric?" Laura asked.

He looked at Celia and heat flashed in his eyes for an instant, a heat laced with hunger and loneliness. It could only have lasted for the space of a heartbeat or less, but in that moment, she saw that he still wanted her as desperately as she wanted him. Flushing, she lowered her eyes.

"I'm sorry," he said to his sister. "I guess I'm just a little restless tonight."

"Why don't you play something for us?" she suggested. "That's usually what you need—to play some music. I haven't heard you play guitar for a long time. I miss it."

Celia bit her lip at the charged silence that met Laura's suggestion. For a moment, she was confused—didn't Laura know about Eric's inability to play? Why would she be so cruel?

Then she caught the flame in Laura's starry blue eyes, a hard flicker of challenge.

"Laura, I don't play guitar anymore. And you know it." A wash of dusky red stained his cheekbones.

Reminded of the day that he'd stumbled on the stairs at the high school, Celia spoke up. "I'll have to let you two settle this between yourselves," she said, dusting her lips with a napkin. "I'm afraid I'm going to have to get home."

Eric's expression of gratitude was ample payment. She gave him a small smile in acknowledgement.

"Oh, do you have to run off?" Laura protested. "We were just getting comfortable."

"I'm afraid I do," Celia said. "It was wonderful. Maybe I can return the favor sometime soon."

Laura nodded, and in her eyes, Celia saw the intelligence and steadiness that lay behind the fluttery, gypsy externals. There was also an entreaty in those eyes, one Celia didn't quite understand.

"Eric, drive her home," Laura said as Celia stood up.

"That's not necessary," Celia protested. "It's a beautiful night. I like walking."

"I'll drive you," he said.

A well of panic rose in her chest at the thought of him sitting in a close space with her, his scent and voice washing over her in the dark. "No," she said, and looked at him, suddenly angry. "I'll walk."

A muscle tightened along his jaw, and he fiddled with a fork idly as he absorbed and deflected her fury. It was as if he knew he deserved it, as if he welcomed it. "I'll walk you out," he said, finally.

Celia lifted her chin. "Thank you again," she said to Laura. "Feel free to drop by. It's still a mess from the flood, but I'd love to see you anytime."

Laura smiled, a curl of pretty lips matched by a secretive, triumphant expression in her eyes. She winked. "I'll see you soon."

Had she missed something? Celia sighed and headed for the door. After coping with one new society after another as a child, she would have imagined the social structure of her own country and people would be a breeze. Nothing could have been farther from the truth. Tonight she felt subtly manipulated, seduced, placed in position in line with someone else's plan. When would she learn the codes around here?

Eric followed her silently out to the porch. "Sure you won't let me drive you?" he asked.

"I'm sure."

"Well, let's go then. It's a long walk."

Celia froze. "I'll be fine, Eric."

"I know." He took her hand with gentleness. "I just want to talk to you in private for a few minutes."

"Will you stop this, Eric?" Mindful of the open screen door and Laura with her secretive smile sitting just beyond, Celia stepped off the porch. "Oh, just drive me." At least it would be over more quickly that way.

She waited while he fetched his keys, then led her around the side of the house to a gray Volvo. "It still smells like river water," he commented as they settled inside. "But at least she's runnin' again."

It was a new car—maybe not brand-new, but no more than a year or two old, and no expense had been spared on the extras. It wasn't the kind of car she would have expected him to drive.

What *had* she expected, then? She frowned, sneaking a glance at his profile, and had to choke back a chuckle at the picture that presented itself. Maybe a truck, old and lovingly maintained, or a Cadillac with fins. She shook her head at the stereotypical offerings.

"What?" he asked.

"It's a nice car," she said, unable to control the puzzled smile curling her lips.

"I love her." He patted the dashboard fondly. "Never has given me a minute of trouble. I looked at some others, but this one just stole my heart."

Celia couldn't help it. She giggled.

He glanced at her. "What did you expect? A broken-down Buick with a V8 and worn paint, the vinyl roof peeling?"

"Something like that," Celia admitted.

"Well," he drawled comfortably, "you're not alone. I get more ribbing over this car than anything else." He made an adjustment on the dashboard. "Truth is, though, I drove a 1969 Buick Skylark for a lot of years and spent more days broken down in little bitty towns than I can count. When I started getting real money, a good car was the first thing I bought."

"I guess having to be on the road all the time it makes sense."

"Not bad for an old country boy without a high school diploma, eh?"

Celia rolled her eyes. "You're so terribly disadvantaged," she said wryly, and realized with a little shock that she meant it. He may not have had the benefit of a formal education, but he was a literate, thinking man. Self-taught, as so many of her own ancestors had been.

In acknowledgment of her point, he chuckled. The sound was rich and hot in the small space. "Don't tell anybody, all right?"

The car purred into the drive toward the farmhouse, and with a pang of dismay, Celia realized she'd done it again—grown comfortable with her prickly, moody drifter, allowed herself to lose her anger and feel pleased to be listening to him. Loving him.

She fell silent as he pulled up in front of the house. A lamp burned in the living room, and another upstairs in the attic, so that she wouldn't have to stumble up the stairs in the dark.

"This is how it looked the night of the storm," Eric said quietly, viewing the house through the windshield. "Warm and safe."

Celia swallowed.

He looked at her. "And it was—just like the woman who took me in."

She saw him leaning closer, his broad shoulders blocking her view as he inclined his head. *Don't,* her mind cried, but her heart was already in her throat.

It might be her last chance.

The thought gave extraordinary clarity to the moment. She noted in acute detail the slope of his cheekbone in the soft moonlight, the cut of his lips thrown into silhouette against the night. He smelled of himself, something hot and male and irresistible. She remembered when he had stood in her kitchen the night of the storm, gulping down popcorn, his lip bleeding—and it seemed impossible that so much had gone between them, that now that same beautiful, roughedged man was bending his head over hers, that she could feel his moist, warm breath whisper over her lips.

So when his mouth touched hers, seductive and hungry and gentle all at once, she nearly shivered at the shock of pleasure it gave her. Her hands flew up to land in the mass of his long, wavy hair, silky and cool and heavy against her fingers. A sound of hunger escaped her throat.

He moved closer, ignoring the limits of bucket seats, tugging her against his chest. His fingers dug into her back with fierce pressure. Celia felt herself spinning away as he kissed her mouth and her chin, her forehead and eyes, talking in between in his dark, raw voice. "I can't help myself, Celia," he whispered as his mouth moved over her cheek. "I can't stop thinking about you, can't stop wanting you."

His mouth touched her temple, her ear, her neck. "I keep telling myself to leave you alone, and I keep breaking that promise and I'm sorry."

The tip of his nose trailed the length of her neck until he nuzzled into the curve of her shoulder. The car's engine still purred. "I wish..."

"Never mind." Celia hugged him, releasing all of her anger, all of her wishes and silly fantasies into the night. "It's all right. Everything is all right." Then, when she could find the courage, she slowly released him. "You'd better get back to your sister," she said.

For an instant, it seemed as if he would not let her go. Then he straightened, nodding.

Celia opened the door, put one foot on the ground, then turned back to him. "Don't leave without telling me goodbye. Please?"

With one finger, he touched her cheek. "I won't."

"Promise?"

"Promise." He lifted his chin toward the house. "Go on, now, before the mosquitoes eat us both alive."

Chapter Thirteen

Eric dreamed of his hands, whole and strong, flying over the strings of his guitar. He dreamed of his mother, pretty and soft and smelling of L'Origan, holding him in her lap.

And he dreamed of Celia—Celia laughing, Celia singing, Celia kissing him in her open, undemanding way.

He awakened to darkness. For a long time, he lay there, staring at the shadows cast by a tree beyond his window. Then, he rose and dressed, took his guitar case from beside the couch and walked out into the damp, near dawn. A path led from behind the house down the bluff that protected it from the river. Jezebel, singing the blues, beckoned him.

Overhead, the sky was indigo, washed clean of stars with the approach of morning. Eric settled on the banks of the river and breathed deeply the coppery scent mixed with pine needles and rich silt and fish. Home.

As a child, he'd not understood that Jezebel had taken his mother. He'd been afraid of storms for a long time, but never of this river. As a boy, he'd spent long, long hours at her side, listening to the musical sound of her stories, imagining she was a benevolent angel sent to keep him safe. He'd run here to escape his uncle's drunken ramblings, to escape the disapproval of the small minority of the town that held him in contempt for his bastard status. He'd come here to practice guitar when Wild Willie had begun to teach him, and it seemed that Jezebel had been as much a teacher as Willie. Steadily she held a beat. Unconditionally, she listened.

So tonight—or rather this morning—he took his guitar from its case with his broken hands. And to Jezebel he played his blues, knowing she would not mind the imperfect sound of his clumsy fingers, that she forgave his ragged transitions and the harsh grate of the wrong pressure of his steel slide.

To Jezebel, he made his offering as dawn filled the sky. To Jezebel he sang his blues, his loss, his sorrow. When he had finished, morning had dawned.

And Eric knew it was time to go.

Celia stood on the back porch, her hands on her hips. The steps were still missing, but she'd found a milk crate to stand in for them until they could be replaced. Beyond, stretching in dark, rich promise, lay her newly planted garden, the rows neatly furrowed as Lynn had instructed, each row sturdily labeled with hand-lettered stakes: popcorn, butterbeans, squash, even watermelon, which Celia had never thought to grow, but Lynn insisted would do very well.

As she surveyed the plot in the lowering late-afternoon light, Celia felt a deep glow of satisfaction. The turning of the ground and the planting itself had been a hard job. Her muscles were weary. A shower had eased most of the soreness, and she was left with a distinct, powerful sense of accomplishment and pride.

In memory, she saw the orderly rows of her grandmother's garden—the popcorn, waving green fronds in a summer wind; the hills of squash; the red flowers of scarlet runners. She smiled. Oh, yes. This was what she'd been made for.

Now that the garden was in, she could begin to repaint the interior of the house. From a catalogue, she'd ordered new furniture out of Dallas, and they had promised delivery at the first of next month. Soon, very soon, her life would be back to normal.

The doorbell rang, echoing faintly into the back through the house. Smoothing a wisp of hair from her face, Celia went to answer it.

Her footfalls echoed in the now-empty rooms. With Lynn's help, she had torn up the soggy, smelly carpets and hauled the ruined furniture out to one side of the house for collection by a clean-up crew—whenever they could get to her. The bare windows gleamed with the washing of vinegar and water she'd given them.

Odd how different everything looked now, Celia thought. She would never have thought she'd want to change anything—but all kinds of ideas were cropping up. A few of the wood pieces were salvageable, and in combination with some of the new things she'd ordered, the rooms would contain the best of old and new. She'd like to leave the big front window bare. It was arched, framed with good mahogany—

Her heart lurched. Standing in that very frame of mahogany, with the graceful branches of the pecan tree giving him a picturesque background, was Eric.

Eric. She touched her hair, feeling suddenly self-conscious, wishing she had bothered to put her makeup on, that she was wearing something other than baggy shorts and an old tank top.

She wished she were wearing something sinful, something that would tempt him to stay.

At the door, she paused, looking up at him through the time-darkened screen. "I guess you've come to tell me you're leaving," she said.

He swallowed, his eyes lost and lonely, and nodded.

She took a breath and pushed the door open, coming outside to stand with him on the warped boards of the porch. "I wish I could convince you to stay," she said honestly—and to her horror, tears thickened her throat.

"I know," he said. His voice was rough and low, as if there were something in his throat, as well.

She looked up at him, and as she had once before, she impressed the details of him into her mind for later reminiscing—the deep hue of his irises, the way he towered over her, the tenderness of his mouth in the hard lines of his face. With a crooked smile, she said, "You're as pretty as a movie star."

He grinned wistfully. "You're one bold woman, you know it?"

Celia nodded, smiling ruefully.

His gaze shifted, lighting on something over her head for a moment before flitting back to her face. "Ah, hell," he said with an air of defeat, and opened his arms. "Come here, will you?"

Celia felt as if she floated toward him, had no conscious memory of telling her feet to step closer. One instant she was standing in her bare feet looking up at him; the next she was crushed in his arms, enveloped in the scent and feel of him. He held her hard, his heart thudding against her ear. And once again she felt the odd, passionate trembling of his arms and legs as he held her, as if he were fighting some great and terrible battle within himself.

She lifted her head to kiss him. He resisted, not actively, but passively, allowing her to touch him, but not returning it. The infinitesimal trembling increased.

"You have to go," she said. "And I have to stay." She let her hands rove over his broad, muscled chest. "Leave me something to remember you by."

"Don't, Celia," he whispered as her hands slid over his sides and tugged his shirt from the waistband of his pants. She kissed him again, a wild hunger building within her. This time, he was not quite so passive. A small groan escaped his throat as her hands found his bare flesh below his shirt—silky, supple skin, hot to the touch.

"I can't sleep sometimes," she whispered, pride gone. His hands slipped downward, almost reluctantly, to cup her bottom and pull her close against his arousal. She opened her mouth against the triangle of skin his shirt exposed. "I think of you touching me and I can't sleep."

"Celia, God help me." Eric grasped her head hard and kissed her, his tongue plunging into her mouth, his teeth bruising her lips. He steered her toward the door and Celia broke away.

"Let's climb the stairs like civilized people this time."

His nostrils flared. "Like hell." He scooped her into his arms. "I'm not feeling civilized," he growled, and lifted his chin in the direction of the door. "Reach down there and open that."

A swelter of arousal made her hands shake as she reached for the handle, and a wild, giddy terror descended as they passed over the threshold.

Eric kicked the door shut behind him, then settled Celia against it and pressed her back against the wood, his hands trapping her wrists at either side of her head.

Deliberately, he pressed into her. "I'm not a real civilized man," he said, and kissed her as if to illustrate, his tongue thrusting deep, his teeth plucking at her lips.

And Celia didn't care. His savage loss of control pleased her, thrilled her—for at last she'd broken through his barriers, every single one of them. In return, she arched against him and moved in invitation, letting go of the inhibitions of a lifetime. Since he held her hands, she shifted and wrapped one leg around him, pulling him closer still, and heard the groan of his pleasure.

This was not the man who remembered to please his woman first, who took pride in his knowledge of "doing it right." Instinctively, she knew his prowess as a lover had been one way of earning approval, of trying to connect his lonely heart with that of another.

Deliberately, she pulled back to look at him square in the eye. Sunlight flashed across the vibrant sapphire irises. "I love you," she said.

He made a sound of pain and kissed her, letting go of her hands. With clumsy haste, he pushed up her blouse as Celia unbuttoned his shirt.

He shuddered at the press of their chests together, and as if he could not help himself, he slipped his hands between them to spread his fingers over her breasts. His broad, scarred palms cradled her. Celia struggled against her need to tumble into the exquisite sensation and concentrated on freeing the stubborn buttons of his jeans. He didn't help her, seemingly lost in the feel of her flesh in his hands, in the taste of her tongue and lips. But when she managed the last button and pushed his jeans from his lean hips, he growled and grabbed her tight.

They tumbled onto the bare floor, covered with only thin scatter rugs. There, in front of the closed door, in a patch of bright yellow sunlight, half-dressed and bruising each other with the violence of their hunger, they joined. His jeans scraped her thighs as he thrust into her, and his shirt fluttered around her sides, but it didn't matter. It didn't matter. They were joined, body and soul. Hands and hearts tangled; lips and minds danced to the bittersweet blues of their parting. And as if to emphasize the perfection, Celia felt her body gathering for its explosion just as Eric made a dark, ragged sound in his throat. Wildly, he kissed her.

Once again there was a magic flaring, an electric shimmer that moved the air around them and passed between them.

Celia opened her eyes. His hair fell over his forehead and neck, mussed by her restless fingers, and a high stain of color flushed his cheekbones. His mouth, parted slightly, was soft and somehow vulnerable. His eyes were closed.

But as she watched, as the pulsing between them ebbed, his lids lifted slowly. A dizziness spun through her, a sense of perfect union that was only rawly expressed through words like *passion* and *hunger* and *love;* a sense of union that made her feel as if the molecular structure of their bodies had come undone, all the atoms spinning together as they made love, only coming back together now, but all mixed, so that parts of her were in Eric and parts of him were in her.

And as he opened his eyes, she saw his tears, a wash of moisture that gave the extraordinary eyes a starry vividness. She pulled him close, cradling his head against her shoulder, pressing her cheek into his hair. "I love you," she whispered. "I love you."

In the deepest heart of the night, Eric awakened. Without words, they'd moved to this attic sanctuary, and there they had stayed without eating or talking—only touching, loving, exploring. He felt like a soldier going off to a war from which he might not return.

Beside him, nestled into the hollow of his shoulder, Celia slept like a child. A fan of silvery hair sprayed over his arm, and her ripe mouth was parted gently. An angel, he thought. So pretty. He trailed a finger over her jaw, lightly so as not to awaken her. Her slim body was curled next to his, trusting and sweet.

In all the hours they had spent together, she had not asked him to stay, not by word or deed. She had not wept or begged, whispered pleas or coerced him. She only stared him straight in the eyes and told him she loved him. Simple. Like Celia. She wasn't afraid to be herself, to tell him her thoughts, to love him—even if he didn't love her in return.

Hollowness struck his heart as he began to ease away from the warmth of her form, a millimeter at a time. She barely stirred. In the darkness he found his clothes, and in darkness he dressed, his throat tight.

When he was ready to go, he paused at the edge of the bed, staring down at the ethereal beauty that was Celia. He thought of braiding her hair and remembered her clenching her fists as the snake crawled over her feet and the way she'd brought him brownies.

But mostly he thought of her steadiness. Upon learning of her career teaching algebra and calculus, he'd thought it was ill suited. Having known her, he knew it was right. There was order in Celia's world, a constancy and reliability he'd never known. She was a woman of her word.

And for that reason, he could not take her with him. Not that she would go, even if he asked. She loved him, and that love had been the most peaceful thing he'd ever known, as soothing as the song of Jezebel on her way to the Gulf. It tempted him to forget his ramblings, tempted him to try to live up to the man she thought she saw. For Celia, he wanted to try.

And as he stood there, filling his eyes with her slight, sleeping form, he felt tears well up in his throat and in his eyes. He felt them come without surprise. He had never cried, not as long as he could remember—not over anything, but with Celia, everything came apart and as he watched her breath sough in and out, the tears spilled over his cheeks, and he let them flow.

He loved her. Loved her as he'd never loved anyone or anything in his life. He loved her for all the things she made him feel, loved her for the light sound of her laughter and her bold kisses and her steadiness. But most of all, he loved her for being absolutely, unapologetically herself.

For one long instant, he realized he was no soldier, only a restless wanderer, that if he wanted to stay, she would welcome him. He nearly knelt, once again, on the soft mattress they had shared and took her into his arms.

But into her stable world he'd brought only chaos. Into the serenity of her simple life he'd brought dark passion and heavy burdens. He had nothing to bring to their union—not even the songs he might once have offered. If he stayed, he would not be giving, he would be taking.

Celia deserved more than that. Much, much more.

He'd told her he would not leave her sleeping, but this time he didn't think he could bear to say goodbye to her open, guileless eyes. With an ache in his chest, he turned and left her, slipping down the stairs like a night wind.

At the car, he looked back to the house, thinking of her father, who had loved Celia only when he had time. Eric would not leave her with that same thought about him.

Reaching into the back seat, he grabbed his guitar. In his hand, the weight was familiar and beloved, and for a moment, he nearly wept again for a different loss, for that loss of his hands. He swallowed.

In the gathering light, he climbed the steps to the porch. He left the guitar where she'd find it, leaving one love to the other, hoping Celia would understand.

The sound of the car driving away awakened Celia. It was still dark and it was that darkness that panicked her, that made her clutch the sheet around herself and race down the stairs to the front door. It was the darkness that made her cry out when she saw the tiny red lights already gone down the road. "Eric!"

The sound of her cry thinned and spread to nothing in the still, morning air. He was gone.

In grief she bowed her head against the screen door, a wide ache exploding through her chest and belly, a grief so deep, she could hardly bear it, could not weep it away. As she struggled to control it, to find some handle to keep the pain at bay, she cursed herself.

Because there had been a part of her that had really believed he would stay. His trembling touch, his warring heart, his need of her last night—he loved her.

She had not let him go without making love to her because she'd hoped one last night together might change his heart, might open his eyes to what could be between them. She had hoped that if she loved him unconditionally enough, his wounds would be lanced and he might begin to believe in himself.

Raising her head, her dry eyes, she saw the guitar on the porch. For one long moment she stared at it, then sheet and all, she stepped outside and picked it up.

Inside, she sank to the floor and opened the case. She'd known he had played, that he loved blues guitar, and she had seen the scars that had rendered him unable to make his music. But she hadn't even seen the instrument upon which he lavished his love. It was made of a hard wood and was finished with a dark blue glaze that made her think of the color of his eyes. It had taken its share of knocks over the years. There were worn places on the neck, places worn away by his thumbs and fingers.

She didn't know the exact logic that had led him to leave it for her, but she could guess. He'd lost his hands, his ability to play this beautiful instrument, and with that loss, he'd lost himself.

It was the most precious thing he owned, this guitar. Celia picked it up and held it against her and it seemed almost an extension of him, as if he'd left her his heart.

Holding the cold weight against her, Celia cursed her father. For Jacob Moon had written this story.

Now it was ending. After finding love he could not accept, the hero would wander far and wide and die a bitter death, while the heroine pined away, alone forever.

"Oh, Daddy!" Celia cried aloud, her heart shattering. "Couldn't you have written just one happy ending?"

Chapter Fourteen

Eric made it as far as New Orleans before his exhaustion caught up with him. It was an almost instantaneous process. One minute he was driving mindlessly, without thought of his destination; the next he was nearly cross-eyed.

At the first exit off the highway, he found a motel, one of a friendly, family chain. In the faceless room, he collapsed without even removing his clothes—just fell onto his belly on the bed and passed out.

When he awakened it was late afternoon of the following day. His hands were stiff with the driving and the lack of movement afterward. They ached. He was dizzy, too, and he remembered he hadn't eaten in a long, long time, save for a couple of oranges purchased at a roadside stand.

He needed food and a shower. He got to his feet and groaned at an ache in his lower back. The room was still and sticky and he flipped on the air conditioner.

His thoughts were frozen—his bodily needs came first. That was what the road did for him, he thought grimly, turning on the shower, kept him so physically miserable he didn't have time to think about anything else.

As he tugged his shirt off, a waft of scent was released from the fabric, a scent of patchouli and roses.

Celia.

He was about to throw it into the corner, but at the last minute, lifted it to his nose. He buried his face in the soft flannel, inhaling deeply, feeling the press of her mouth upon his own, the give of her pliant body, the sound of her laughing....

Instead of throwing the shirt aside, he folded it and wrapped the plastic shower cap around it to preserve the precious scent.

The shower and a solid meal eased most of his physical discomfort although his back still ached vaguely. Long road trips, because he'd made so many of them, had begun to make his back ache—one of the reasons the Volvo with its heated seats had been so appealing.

Outside the restaurant where he'd eaten, he paused. It was summer. It was night. It was New Orleans. Somewhere, somebody was playing the blues.

He found them in a close little bar near the levee— a quartet playing Delta style. Eric knew the guitarist from a long way back when both had been perfecting their licks for just enough money to buy their beer for the night and a little breakfast the next day. On a break, Eric bought him a drink, and they hunched together over the whiskey, laughing about old times.

"So where you been, man?" Davis asked. "I heard about that accident, but you plain dropped outta sight."

Eric lifted a shoulder. "Just been putting things back together."

"You written anything new lately?"

"A little," Eric replied, thinking of the song for his sister and the harmonica pieces that had been flitting through his mind.

"Come on up and share 'em," Davis said.

For the first time in two years, Eric was tempted. He looked around the dark, softly smoky room, feeling the old longing to share the blues with a room full of people.

Davis waited, and Eric suddenly felt a swell of rightness—this old friend would know where to fill in with his guitar while Eric sang or played his harp. The music would not be exactly what he thought it was now; the crowd and Davis and even Eric's mood would influence it. It was time. Giving Davis a nod, Eric said, "Yeah. I'd like that."

And so it was that he found himself on stage for the first time since the night Retta died. For a moment, as the band assembled around him, Eric felt a little awkward without the ever-present shield of his guitar. Then he tugged his harmonica from his pocket and settled on a stool, and the stage fright passed.

They started with one of the pieces Eric had written a long time ago, the same song Willie had sung at the club in Gideon: "Jezebel's Blues." Hearing the words now, Eric had to smile at the memory of the homesick boy who'd written them. It was odd to hear someone else play the slow guitar he'd always played, but there was satisfaction in meshing the harmonica with that guitar, in weaving together the old with the new.

After a time, Davis nodded at him and Eric leaned into the microphone to sing. At the sound of his voice, a whoop sailed out from the floor and he stopped, grinning, then started again and kept going in spite of the whistles and catcalls from the crowd. He fell into the singing, into the songs, old songs and new ones, songs he had written and songs he hadn't. Behind him and with him, Davis played guitar and sang harmony. Even Eric could hear how good they sounded together, and he wondered how it was they'd never blended their voices before this.

They played until they were sweaty with the humid air and exertion, sang until Eric was hoarse. And when they would have quit, the crowd whooped and hollered for one more. Just one more.

Davis nudged him. "Do your new one," he said. "I'll follow you."

Eric paused, then settled on the stool and lifted the harmonica to his lips, bending into it. He coaxed a slow, mournful pull of notes, hearing the nights he'd sat on Laura's porch, wondering if she were alive or dead. It wasn't what he'd meant to play, but years of living by intuition told him to go with it. He played the notes he'd composed in Gideon, first in Celia's attic, then on Laura's porch and finally on the banks of Jezebel that last morning.

There was loss and grief and despair, the long, long story of his life, the story of things never ending right, but always, always going foul. There was the ache of a motherless child and the pain of never settling. Davis's guitar picked out a melancholy key and his slide whined over the strings in the old Delta style.

When Eric was sure the guitar had found the pattern he needed for background, he let the harp take him in another direction. Through the sorrow now wove moonlight, silver and soft—the sound of a fey slender woman, the sound of her laughing into Eric's melancholy and breaking it up.

When it was over, Eric leaned into the mike. "That was for Celia," he said, and climbed down from the stool.

The crowd let the band break. Someone dropped coins into the jukebox, and Eric blotted his face with a handkerchief. "Thanks, man," he said to Davis. "It's been too damned long."

Davis chuckled and drank deeply of a glass of water. "You keep up on that harp, you'll be another Sonny Terry one of these days."

Eric made a dismissive grimace. "Listen, I was back home for a while, and there's a boy named James whose going to be somebody on guitar. Another year, he'll be ready to try his wings. I'd like to get him out here before the summer's through to play a night or two and get his feet wet."

Davis smiled. "Tell you what—I'll make you a deal. You write some words to that piece you just played and let me work out something to get it recorded, and I'll see your boy gets what he needs.''

"You got it.''

"I want you on harmonica,'' Davis added as Eric headed off stage.

He lifted a hand. "I'll be around.''

The satisfaction of his playing and singing, the pleasure of letting the blues flow through him lasted until Eric opened the door of his faceless motel room in the middle of the night.

He went in and closed the door quietly so as not to awaken the vacationing families all around him.

It was so quiet. No birds signing, no cats fighting, no river rushing by in a soothing song. Faintly over the hum of the air conditioner came the sounds of trucks on the freeway. A lonely sound. He tugged off his boots and socks and flipped on the television and set it to a cable station playing movies through the night. But it didn't provide the kind of noise he was looking for and he flipped it off again.

There was no smell here, either. No scent of pine or frying bacon; no fishy odor hanging like a ghost in reminder of a good meal; no coppery scent of water or rich earth. Only a faint trace of some astringent cleaner and freshly washed linen—pleasant enough, but without character.

He dug in his backpack for another orange, some Oreos and his old standby, the rubber-banded paperback copy of Jacob Moon's *Song of Mourning*. It had helped him pass more than one lonely night.

After a trip to the soda-pop machine for a can of cola, he sprawled on the bed and began to read. It was a little tougher this time to settle in. There were intrusions now. His life had shifted dramatically since the last time he'd tried his homesick cure. Tonight instead of getting lost in the story, he kept thinking of reading the original manuscript. He remembered the tiny changes that had been made in the publishing process, shifts that aligned each word with every other word.

Celia's face kept appearing as he read over the words: Celia laughing at him as he told his sad story; Celia weeping because she missed her father; Celia tossing her head with a wicked smile as she pinned him against the mattress with her lithe, lovely body.

But he'd spent more years than he could count trying to forget things that gave him pain. He concentrated. By the third chapter, he was firmly anchored in the Gideon of his childhood, and he immersed himself in the old magic.

It was a story about a boy from the wrong side of the tracks who fought like hell to be somebody, only to die a tragic, early death believing the worst everyone had ever said about him. It was a simple and familiar tale, and he read it less for the story than for the mood of home that ran through it like a song. Like the blues.

But tonight, as he read, Eric felt an embarrassed little shock over his identification with the main character. It seemed uncomfortably melodramatic.

Celia's words wafted through his mind: No wonder you like my daddy's books. *They're written about your life, aren't they?*

In a way, the book was the story of his life, and particularly since this last trip home, it rang true. But as he read, he grew uncomfortable.

For every time the young man had a chance, he sabotaged himself. Eric had always *known* that, known that half the reason the character died tragically was his own fault. This time he felt a distinct annoyance at the hero, particularly when there was a woman in his corner, a woman who honestly loved him, who could have healed him if he'd given her a chance.

Whenever you get over feeling sorry for yourself, you know where to find me.

With a sigh, he put the book down, pursing his lips as a new angle of the novel settled in, obvious as the nose on his face if he'd just come out of his brooding long enough to see it. *Song of Mourning* was a morality tale. It had a lesson to teach. Because Moon had been the writer he was, a member of the school of obscure lessons, it was a fable.

Eric chuckled, amazed he'd been so stupid all these years. The moral was simple. Believe. That's all. Believe in yourself.

Jacob Moon had known a bit about the cruelty of small towns, Southern or not. He'd known about the fierce, biting gossip that occupied the minds of little people in a fishbowl where almost nobody had any money to spend, where the long bitterness of endless poverty lashed out at anyone who dared to be happy.

Moon had also exiled himself from the one place he loved. It made Eric sad to realize that, to realize that Jacob had been buried unimaginable miles from the soil in which his roots had been planted. Away from Gideon, Jacob had been lost, so lost that he'd killed himself rather than go on when faced with the loss of his wife.

Self-destruction.

Eric felt suddenly dizzy. He didn't know—guessed that he probably never would know—why Jacob Moon had left Gideon forever. He could only see the end result.

Self-destruction.

That terrible night when Eric had stomped his foot hard on the accelerator, thus ending the only life he'd ever known and killing someone else was forever etched upon his heart.

He flashed back to that night, to the jeers of Retta from the audience, to the biting comments she had made in the car before the accident. He had seen so much of himself in her. In those moments before he'd stomped his foot down on the accelerator, he'd been thinking both of their lives were a joke. In fury and bleak despair, he had committed his own act of self-destruction.

He would pay the price for the rest of his life. He would always regret that he had been unable to save Retta, that indirectly, he had killed her.

But the clock, no matter how much he wished, could not ever be turned back. It moved only forward.

With a sense of extraordinary clarity, he picked up the book. Firmly, he wrapped the rubber band around it and settled it among his clothes in his backpack.

He was homesick as hell. He was always homesick when he left Gideon. He'd only left to begin with because his love of the blues had required him to leave its safe arms to seek his fortune. Over the years, to ease that ache, he'd convinced himself he hated it.

There were things he hated. The small-mindedness of some of its people, surely. The poverty that was undeniably part of the little town, that too. But he'd seen small minds in his travels. And poverty in the country was a far sight better than poverty in the city. At least there was clean air to breathe and the sounds of birds in the trees. Poor in the country meant there was still some dignity, some fresh food that didn't come from the government. No machine guns in the country, either.

He'd sought his fortune. And he'd found it.

His sins and losses, when laid out side by side, balanced out pretty clean. He'd lost his hands and the guitar that had saved him. But he still had the blues in his voice, in his harp and in his soul, where the blues lived anyway.

The face of a fey and teasing woman washed through his mind. He smiled in longing and love. For she was the true source of his homesickness this time. Celia was home. Celia was love. Celia was hope and strength and honor. Celia believed. In Eric, in herself, in Gideon. Her belief had flat dead-ended his own self-destructive bent, had opened his eyes to what should have been obvious for a long, long time.

He hitched the backpack over his shoulder for the last time, turned off the light and closed the door with a tight click behind him. A soft dawn pushed through the wide New Orleans sky.

Only one problem remained. Eric still had no idea what he would do with himself, how he would occupy his time. He needed to work somehow. As he drove, he examined the possibilities.

He was whistling "Jezebel's Blues" softly between his teeth, watching out for a Plymouth barreling up on him from behind, when the answer struck him. The Plymouth passed him in a whoosh of sound, the wind currents buffeting the Volvo, but Eric hardly noticed.

The idea struck like a two-by-four between the eyes, clear and perfect and so obvious, Eric wondered how the hell he'd managed to avoid seeing it for so long.

He laughed out loud and pressed his foot just a little harder to the gas pedal. Lord, it was good to be going home.

Chapter Fifteen

On Saturday morning, Celia donned her oldest clothes, caught back her hair in a braid and with great satisfaction, began to paint the living room. Lynn had loaned her a small, portable radio, which Celia tuned to a rock-'n'-roll station out of Dallas.

Humming along, she painted cheerfully. A portable fan kept the humid air from choking her completely, and she made a resolve to look into real airconditioning. Romance aside, the muggy, hot air would not be good for her new furniture, and what good would all her daddy's money do sitting in a bank?

She'd spent the last four days in a flurry of activity, working in the house and garden like a madwoman to keep her thoughts of Eric at bay. Laura had stopped by one afternoon, just to chat she'd said—but Celia had the feeling Laura was checking up on her, making sure she was all right. Upon seeing the furious activity Celia was engaged in, Laura had commented wryly that she guessed Celia would be fine.

The memory brought a frown to Celia's lips. She slapped pale salmon paint on the walls, wondering if Laura had expected to come by and find her fading away in grief.

Celia snorted. Fat chance. It might take her a while—even she acknowledged that much—but her life would be good and fine and full because she deserved it. She had worked hard to settle in Gideon, had worked hard to form friendships and learn the customs of the locals.

A pluck of sorrow tugged at her chest. She missed Eric. Maybe she'd always miss him. But she didn't regret knowing him, didn't regret the time and love she'd given him. At the very, very beginning, she had known she couldn't hold him.

But that didn't mean she wouldn't go on. Her great passion and only love was Eric—she accepted that. As long as she lived, she would hold the memory of his lonely eyes in her heart. Always, a piece of her would grieve at the loss of what might have been. It was tragic, for both of them.

That didn't mean her life would end. One day she would find a man she could like and respect and trust to help her raise children. There were all kinds of ways to make marriages work. There was bound to be a man out there who, like Celia, had given away the best of his heart, but would be willing to build a life with her from the rest.

She bit her lip hard at the thought, willing herself not to cry, a feeling reinforced when she heard a car in the front of the house. She would *not* allow Lynn or Laura or anyone else to see her grief.

Resolutely, Celia climbed the ladder to begin the upper half of the painting. Footsteps crossed the porch. Heavy footsteps.

Curious, Celia paused in her work to look over her shoulder. The ceilings were ten feet high, however, and all she could see was a pair of worn brown boots, the most common by far of all the shoes men in this town wore.

But in spite of herself, she dropped the paintbrush. It fell all the way to the plastic tarp on the floor and landed with a splat, spraying pale pink paint in a little arc all around it.

Just as it hit, the booted person rapped hard on the screen door. Celia jumped and cursed. She started to climb down, but the door opened.

Eric stepped through. She froze for a moment, unprepared. His shirt hung unbuttoned around his chest and a shadow of unshaven beard darkened his strong jaw. He looked up at her a moment without saying a word, his vivid blue eyes shining with a light Celia had never seen in them before.

Stung, dizzy with his presence and the roiling emotions it brought up, she said harshly, "What? Did you forget your guitar?"

"No," he said. "I forgot my woman."

Without her paintbrush, Celia had no prop, but she faked it. She brushed a lock of hair from her face with violently trembling fingers. "I don't know who that might be, but this woman is staying right here."

He smiled, a slow, sexy, devastating smile. "So am I."

A flush of fury raced through her. She wanted to slap that sure smile from his face, kick him hard to hurt him, do something to even the score. Instead, she slammed her hand against the ladder. "Damn you!" she whispered.

He sobered and she saw the flash of understanding in his eyes. So quickly that she had no defence, he crossed the room and pulled her down from the ladder, pulled her hard against his broad chest. "You want to beat me up, don't you?"

She punched his shoulder, trying to resist the opiate of his scent, that lush smell of hot nights and passion. He held her as she struggled, accepting the punch as his due. "Go ahead," he murmured. "Hit me as hard as you can. I deserve it, Celia. I really do. I know it. I'm sorry."

But somehow, he was kissing her, his mouth tender and sweet and tasting of oranges. All the fight left her. She made a little cry against his mouth and suddenly there were hot tears flowing over her face, tears of release she couldn't halt, tears she could taste on his mouth.

"Oh, Celia, sugar, I'm sorry," he said, and pulled her close, so close she could barely breathe. "I'm as dumb as a mule about things sometimes." His hand stroked her hair, and Celia pressed her face into the shelf of his collarbone, breathing in his strength and tenderness.

He lifted his head and she saw him swallow. "There were a lot of things I could get over," he said in his rough voice. "You weren't one of them." He cupped her face in one broad, scarred palm. "I love you, sugar."

Celia closed her eyes. To her dismay, she was so dizzy she felt very close to a swoon. For one long moment, she let his words and his touch and his apologies sink in. Then with a breath, she stepped out of the circle of his arms.

"I spent my whole childhood with people who were up one minute, down the next," she said. "Brooding, stormy, creative people." She licked her lips. "I love you, too, Eric, but I can't face that kind of craziness for the rest of my life."

A glimmer lit his eyes in the dark face, giving them an almost neon hue. His lips curled into a seductive smile, and almost too casually, he settled his hands on his hips. Celia felt her breath catch on an instant, furious wave of desire. She stepped back with one foot.

His grin widened and he looked for all the world like a picture on an album cover, like a movie clip, like every erotic promise ever made.

"This isn't fair," she said.

He stepped closer.

Celia stepped back.

"What's not fair, Celia?" he asked, cocking an eyebrow. His dark voice rumbled over her spine in a moonshine rush of heat.

For an instant she realized what he must be like on stage, singing, all his charisma unleashed and turned toward the audience. Overwhelming.

In a panic she turned away, covering her ears and closing her eyes. She had to *think*.

When he grabbed her playfully from behind, Celia yelped. A rich, low chuckle sounded close to her ear. He kissed her neck. "All's fair in love and war, sugar." His big hands moved deliberately on her belly, circling. "And I told you I've got my own little area of expertise. Remember?"

Celia shuddered. This was a side of him she'd rarely seen, the man who had fished on the banks of Jezebel and teased her in the attic and . . .

He bent his head to her neck again, and helplessly, Celia turned in his arms. His eyes glimmered with humor, and the dark, hard planes of his face were gentle. "Kiss me like you do," he whispered. "You had me from the very first time."

Celia lifted her face, but he did the kissing. It was a kiss like no other, slow and long and deep—like the blues. There was no trembling in his limbs now, no war he fought with himself—just a pure and direct focus on Celia's mouth, and he played it with the same expertise he brought to the harmonica. His hands played her body, slipping here and there, sliding over heated centers now, tickling cool places into flames. He pressed her into his hips.

"You drive me crazy, Celia," he growled. "I want to be inside you day and night, and when I'm not, that's what I'm thinking about." His hand slid around to her breast. "I want to taste that pretty pink nipple, because it was made for my mouth, and you know it."

"Eric," she protested. "Sex doesn't solve anything."

He suckled her neck. "That's not sex, Celia." Slowly, he was backing up, pulling her with him toward the stairs. "I've had enough to know better."

His tone sobered, and he lifted his head, touching her lips with his thumb. "This is love so big, it makes me cry." He swallowed. "It's something so deep, I could never find anything to fill that hole no matter how far and wide I ran."

Now it was Celia who trembled, in fear and hope and hunger. His face was inches from her own, so close, she could see the traces of the scar he'd got on his lip in the flood.

And still his words poured from him. "I love you, Celia Moon, with all my heart and soul and mind— but the way it comes out is that I want to touch you, be so deep in you that we get all mixed up. You felt it. I know you did."

"What about—"

"Shh." He kissed her. "I haven't given you much reason, but I wish you'd trust me this one time. Come with me, upstairs. Let me make love to you like we have forever, just this once. Then we can talk all day."

Celia swayed, drunk on his voice, on his words, on the hope he promised. He lifted her gently, and they climbed the stairs like civilized people.

"Now, see?" he said later. "That wasn't so bad, was it?"

Celia laughed. "Feeling that good is bound to be sinful," she said ruefully.

He traced a circle on her tummy. "Not if it's blessed by a preacher."

"What do you mean?"

He swallowed, and a dark flush heated his cheekbones. He frowned. "What do you *think* I mean?"

"I don't know. Why don't you tell me?"

He laughed, the third time in as many hours. Celia thought with a shock that she'd hardly heard him laugh that much in three weeks. "Okay. Let me back up a minute."

Covering herself with the sheet demurely, she nodded. "I'm listening."

Eric took a deep breath "I write songs," he said. "That's where the money is and always has been for me. I don't need to wander anymore to build up a name and contacts for myself." He watched his hand on her tummy, drawing restless circles. "I thought when I lost my hands I lost the blues forever, Celia. What really happened was that I lost myself, because my whole life was built on sand."

Celia waited, a ripple of hope growing within her.

"My rock is Gideon. I'm so homesick when I leave here, I'm crazy with it. I got out there on the road and I missed you so bad in five minutes, I had to make myself miserable physically to forget you."

"But Eric—"

"Wait a second." He licked his lip. "I want to marry you, Celia. In a little white church and you in a lace dress, with bridesmaids and a piano player. All of it. I want to do it right."

She was shaking her head before he even finished. "You can't do that to yourself, Eric. You love the blues—they're your whole life. I don't want you to make a choice like that."

He laughed. "I'm not making a choice. That's what I'm trying to tell you. Anytime I want, I can show up in any club from here to Charlotte and play or sing. New Orleans is close. We can pop over there for a night or two whenever we want to. Whenever I need to." He grinned and came a little closer. "Besides, I have a plan."

"What plan?"

"It's a surprise." He grabbed her and pinned her beneath him. His thick glossy hair fell forward around his face. "You gonna give in now, or do I have to torture you?"

He's happy, Celia thought, looking at Eric's beautiful face and form. Her restless, lonely drifter was happy. The shadows were gone from his eyes, the lines of strain from his face. And she, Celia Moon, had done that.

"That depends," she said with a slow, wicked smile, "upon exactly what torture you had planned."

He dived toward her, grabbing her with the playfulness he'd always hidden, his mouth smiling, his eyes dancing. "You think it's funny now, but we'll see how you feel in a minute."

Celia laughed, shrieking playfully as he illustrated his luscious torture. When she felt as if she would explode, she grabbed his hands. "I give," she cried breathlessly, "I give!"

He lifted his head and his eyes were hot and soft. "You gave me back my life," he whispered, and kissed her. Tangling with her, arms and legs and sheets and lips and hair, he groaned softly. "Oh, Celia, sugar, it's so good to be home."

Chapter Sixteen

It was possibly the biggest celebration the small town of Gideon, Texas, had ever seen—people had been talking about it for weeks in the diner and the Piggly-Wiggly and the bait shop. A Blues Extravaganza to celebrate the opening of a new blues club.

Laura, Lynn and Celia crossed the gravel parking lot together just after dark. Celia wore the sinful black dress that had once belonged to her grandmother and black stockings and high-heeled shoes. Lynn and Laura were similarly dressed, and as the trio made its way toward the doors, more than one man's whistle sounded out in the steamy sir.

Twenty feet from the door, Celia paused, clutching her stomach. All around her were cars with license plates from all over the South, Louisiana to North

Carolina. A crowd spilled outside, white and black, young and old, every single one of them dressed to the nines.

"What's wrong?" Laura asked, stopping in concern.

"I had no idea he was so famous," Celia whispered, a nervous wavering in her belly.

Laura smiled and lifted one careless eyebrow. "Now you know."

Celia took a deep breath, her mind a kaleidoscopic whirl as she saw hordes of paparazzi of a dozen European cities on the sidewalks. She remembered getting a black eye from the elbow of an overeager photographer once. Jet set. That had been her parents.

This was a completely different kind of crowd. There was an almost palpable aroma of anticipation of the music that was coming, a fervid excitement. And Eric, her Eric, had put it all together.

Shortly after his return to Gideon, he had spent several days engaged in secret errands. Finally, with his plans firmly in motion, he revealed his idea.

And for weeks he'd thrown himself into the preparations for this night, the grand opening of his blues club. Celia smiled to herself. All the suppressed energy she had sensed in him came out as he made dozens of phone calls, ordering supplies, and chairs and tables, calling musicians he knew, who knew others, who agreed it was time for a major blowout.

"I've never even seen him perform," Celia said helplessly.

Laura laughed. "Oh, honey. You love him now." She grabbed her arm. "Just wait."

The club had been given a fresh coat of whitewash and a sign outside proclaimed its name proudly. Inside, a bevy of bartenders poured beer from taps and clacked ice into glasses, and a flurry of waitresses tried to keep up with orders. A ripple of excitement rushed through Celia.

Just as the three women took their seats, the first cluster of musicians ambled onto the stage. The young man Celia had seen at Eric's house picked up a guitar, and the reed-thin old sax player grinned at him. A piano player Celia didn't know sat down. The crowd started to cheer and holler and whoop, its excitement drowning out the sounds of the warm-up from the stage.

At last Eric came forward, smiling easily as he lifted a hand. Celia felt her stomach flip over. She clutched her fists in her lap. This was the real Eric, the man she had seen lurking in the magnetic charisma that was nearly too large to be contained in even this big room.

And everyone knew it. There were genuine screams as he bent over the microphone—piercing whistles and roaring from both men and woman. He started to talk, but was drowned out. With a wry half smile, he glanced at James.

Lost in the audience, Celia stared at Eric. He wore his simple uniform of jeans and boots and a chambray shirt. His hair was too long, but it gave him just the right aura of rakishness to go along with his heart-stopping smile.

When the crowd showed no signs of settling down, he bent over the mike and whistled back. "Hush, y'all or we'll never get to anything."

In a daze Celia heard him introduce the various blues greats who would be singing and playing this evening. He thanked Gideon, to more shouts and hollers, and promised the town would be a center of the blues if he had anything to do with it.

Then he stepped back, winked at James and they eased into the first song.

Celia recognized the notes instantly. They were the same ones Eric had played in her attic the night they had talked of his childhood. Woven in were the bits and pieces she had heard him playing on Laura's porch, the melancholy notes that called up visions of lonely graveyards.

Eric played the harmonica on the intro, then bent his head and began to sing.

It was a song about a man, restless and hungry, who traveled far away from home; about a man who sought the truth of his life, over and over, and never found it because the truth was left behind in a little town by a river that sang magical songs. It was lyrical and mythical and folksy, like all good blues.

It was the story of Jacob Moon. As Celia met Eric's eyes, watching him through a blur of tears, she thought it was the finest tribute her father could have had—a blues song written in his honor. It made her cry. Laura squeezed Celia's hand. Celia looked up to see that Laura's eyes were filled with tears, as well. "I never thought he'd play again, Celia," Laura said, and she wetly kissed Celia's cheek.

When Eric finished, he smiled across the room. Celia shook her head and raised her hands to clap with the rest of the crowd, even stuck her fingers into her mouth and whistled, smiling in pride at him.

"Before we move on, I'd like y'all to meet somebody." He lifted his hand and gestured toward Celia. "Come on up here, sugar."

Celia blushed and widened her eyes at him, warningly, shaking her head infinitesimally.

He grinned at the crowd. "She's shy." He jumped off the stage and cut straight through the tables to her, amid chuckles and shouts and whistles of approval.

Celia set her jaw and vowed silently to kill her husband when she got him home. His laughing eyes told her he knew it and that he'd welcome the tussle. He grabbed her hand and tugged her to her feet. "This beautiful ray of sunshine is my wife, and you have her to thank for this night." He looked at Celia, his eyes shining. His voice dropped to a more sober note. "Because if it wasn't for her, I wouldn't be here."

And right there, in front of hundreds of people, in front of Laura and Lynn, who were cheering along with everyone else, he kissed her.

Celia swallowed, flushing as the crowd clapped with enthusiasm.

"Now I'm going to get out of the way and let some other folks play." He nodded toward James. "I have to dance with my woman."

James fell into a song Celia recognized as Eric pulled her from the stage to join others beginning to mill out onto the floor for a slow dance.

He took her in his arms. "Remember this song?"

Celia nodded. "You walked out on it the last time."

"'Jezebel's Blues,'" he said. "It was the first song I wrote." He pulled her close. "Thank you for giving it back to me."

Celia smiled. "It wasn't me that gave it back."

His clear, untroubled eyes met hers. For a moment they were puzzled, then he grinned in understanding. "I guess we owe old Jezebel quite a bit, don't we?"

"You owe her another song, I think," Celia said.

He pushed her head into the crook of his shoulder. "I'll write her a whole ream of songs."

Celia just settled close, feeling his voice humming through his chest, hearing the celebration of the blues in the tapping feet and hazy pictures dancing all over the room.

"I love you," she whispered, and knew she meant the blues and Gideon and the river, but most of all her precious, beautiful drifter, whose loneliness was gone forever.

The notes of the music drifted out the door to mingle with the song of the river, who sang peacefully between her banks, mollified. A bright sign shone over the door of the club, and its reflection shimmered in her dark waters.

Jezebel's.

*   *   *   *   *

Silhouette
SPECIAL EDITION™

It takes a very special man to win

That
SPECIAL
Woman!

She's friend, wife, mother—she's you! And beside each Special Woman stands a wonderfully *special* man. It's a celebration of our heroines—and the men who become part of their lives.

Look for these exciting titles from Silhouette Special Edition:

January   BUILDING DREAMS by Ginna Gray
Heroine: Tess Benson—a woman faced with single motherhood who meets her better half.

February   HASTY WEDDING by Debbie Macomber
Heroine: Clare Gilroy—a woman whose one spontaneous act gives her more than she'd ever bargained for.

March   THE AWAKENING by Patricia Coughlin
Heroine: Sara McAllister—a woman of reserved nature who winds up in adventure with the man of her dreams.

April   FALLING FOR RACHEL by Nora Roberts
Heroine: Rachel Stanislaski—a woman dedicated to her career who finds that romance adds spice to life.

Don't miss THAT SPECIAL WOMAN! each month—from some of your special authors! Only from Silhouette Special Edition!

NORA ROBERTS

Love has a language all its own, and for centuries flowers have symbolized love's finest expression. Discover the language of flowers—and love—in this romantic collection of 48 favorite books by bestselling author Nora Roberts.

Two titles are available each month at your favorite retail outlet.

In December, look for:

Partners, Volume #21
Sullivan's Woman, Volume #22

In January, look for:

Summer Desserts, Volume #23
This Magic Moment, Volume #24

Collect all 48 titles
and become fluent in
THE LANGUAGE of LOVE

Silhouette®
™

VOWS
A series celebrating marriage
by Sherryl Woods

To Love, Honor and Cherish—these were the words that three
generations of Halloran men promised their women they'd live
by. But these vows made in love are each challenged by the
tests of time....

In October—Jason Halloran meets his match in *Love #769*;
In November—Kevin Halloran rediscovers love—with his
wife—in *Honor #775*;
In December—Brandon Halloran rekindles an old flame in
Cherish #781.

These three stirring tales are coming down the aisle toward
you—only from Silhouette Special Edition!

**Starting in January
be on the lookout for**

MAVERICKS

LISA JACKSON'S
MAVERICK MEN

They're wild...they're woolly...and
they're as rugged as the great outdoors.
They've never needed a woman before,
but they're about to meet their matches....

HE'S A BAD BOY (#787)—January
HE'S JUST A COWBOY (#799)—March
HE'S THE RICH BOY (#811)—May

All men who just won't be tamed!
From Silhouette Special Edition.

SEMAV-1

AMERICAN HERO

Every month in Silhouette Intimate Moments, one fabulous, irresistible man is featured as an American Hero. You won't want to miss a single one. Look for them wherever you buy books, or follow the instructions below and have these fantastic men mailed straight to your door!

In September:
MACKENZIE'S MISSION by Linda Howard, IM #445

In October:
BLACK TREE MOON by Kathleen Eagle, IM #451

In November:
A WALK ON THE WILD SIDE by Kathleen Korbel, IM #457

In December:
CHEROKEE THUNDER by Rachel Lee, IM #463

AMERICAN HEROES—men you'll adore, from authors you won't want to miss. Only from Silhouette Intimate Moments.

INTIMATE MOMENTS®
™ *Silhouette* ®